# Carolina
# Crossroads

_Mary Margaret_
_Enjoy_ _Love you_
_Janet_

# Carolina
# Crossroads

### By H. K. Van Nostrand

Pentland Press, Inc.
England • USA • Scotland

PUBLISHED BY PENTLAND PRESS, INC.
5122 Bur Oak Circle, Raleigh, North Carolina 27612
United States of America
919-782-0281

ISBN 1-57197-207-2
Library of Congress Control Number: 99-75940
Copyright © 2000 H. K. Van Nostrand

Printed in the United States of America

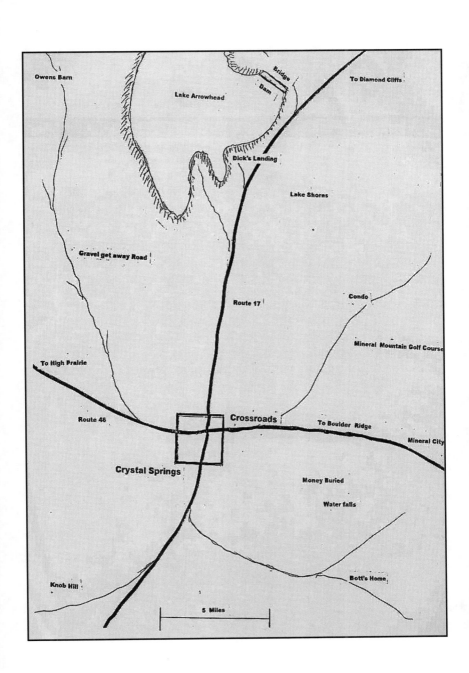

# One

"Yes, I am, I'm going to rob a bank!" Charlie Carson confirmed the shocking answer that he had already given his second son. With a slight air of intolerance, he threw his suitcase on the bed and began to pack.

"Oh, come on, Dad, at your age you couldn't rob a candy store," commented his second son John. "You're always teasing us."

"Don't underestimate me. Just because I'll be eighty this year and have had a quadruple bypass, don't count on me being all washed up," replied Charlie as he neatly packed his bag. "The one conclusion that I've made is that I cannot live with any of my three grown children." After all, Charlie's children were now married and had children of their own. And Charlie knew that he could never adjust to their lives. His disgust at this moment was not the result of a poor previous life, but because his future life looked dull and uninteresting. All he could envision was several years of monotonous rocking in front of a TV until at last death would overtake him.

At this moment, the phone rang and Charlie picked it up to hear his oldest son, Bill, wishing him bon voyage. "Have you figured out where you're going?" asked Bill.

"Yeah, first I'll go to the time-share at the Mineral Mountain Golf Course; then maybe to Crystal Springs or High Prairie," answered Charlie, "I'll call you from time to time to let you know what's happening to me."

"Hell, Dad, this is crazy! What are you going to do up there all alone? Why don't you come stay with us? We can . . ."

"What am I going to do?" Charlie interrupted with vigor, "I'll tell you what I'm going to do. I'm going to start a new life! I'm going to rob a bank in North Carolina!"

Bill chuckled out loud, for he knew that his father often did things that others wouldn't dare do. Usually, they weren't dangerous or illegal. Bill reminded his father of the time when Bill and his brother, Johnny, were in their very early teens and were having a water fight in the shower with each other. And how Charlie silently crept into the bathroom with a bucket of ice cold water and dumped the entire amount on the two boys. Of course, the boys screamed and chased after Charlie, who they thought had slipped out the back door of the house. The boys thought they could catch their father but he had tricked them and once they were out the door, Charlie slammed it shut and locked it. The boys were caught outside in the nude. They ran around to the side door only to find Charlie had already locked it. Then it was a mad dash to the front door to get there before their father did. As they rounded the corner of the house, Mrs. Shaffner from across the street was getting into her car. The boys had to wait until she left the area. Unfortunately, they were too late as Charlie clicked the lock on the front door. Both boys scrambled to get a couple of palm fronds to cover themselves. They tried to be as inconspicuous as possible, but naturally, at that moment, several cars drove in front of the house. Charlie's wife, Ethyl, spotted the embarrassing predicament of her two sons, so she secretly opened the side door to let them back in. Then it became a free-for-all wrestling match between Charlie and his two sons with Ethyl as referee.

Bill laughed again, for he figured that this was another trick. He believed that his father was just trying to torment his sons once again. But on the other hand, Bill knew that his father needed to change his life since Ethyl had recently passed on after a long battle with cancer. "Now listen, Dad," said Bill, "don't go up there to North Carolina and steal a lot of money just so you can leave us a huge legacy. There are many different directions that you can pursue that would be legal and moral, especially up there in the mountains. Don't forget to take your golf clubs and don't get into any trouble. You're too damned old to spend time in some mountain jail."

"I'm sorry to hear you say that, 'cause I felt sure that you'd come up to scold me, first, and then to bail me out." Both men laughed as they hung up the phone.

After farewells with each member of his family, Charlie fell asleep, exhausted from the variety of advice that had been offered. Everything from moving in with one family to selling his mortgage-free home and then moving into a retirement home. He disliked the idea of moving in with strangers. His future was certainly limited and bleak. All of the advice meant that he must now give up his independence in order to yield to the dominance of others, and on their turf, not his. Charlie was convinced that he must now shed the mantle of being the senior member of the family. He wanted to be a contemporary, not the patriarch.

The next morning, Charlie rose early, jumped in his rather old looking car, and turned north toward North Carolina. It was almost a relief, for he was putting all of his problems and obligations behind him. His thoughts were primarily about his extensive family. Bill, his eldest son, was married to a very wholesome-looking lady with very conservative, old-fashioned ideas.

John, the second son, was the biggest and strongest. He was still single, but at times, he would live with one girlfriend, then she'd be gone and another would take her place. The last girl always seemed to be more beautiful than any of the previous. John gained a lot of respect from his peers just because of his size. He gave the appearance of a gentle giant.

Susan, the one beloved daughter, had assumed the position that had been occupied by her mother. It was fitting that she occupy the center of this family for she had the intelligence, the logic, and, above all, the stability. Her immediate family was still expanding rapidly—two boys, one girl, and one on the way. Charlie was extremely proud of his daughter, mainly because she took such good care of him, and also because her beauty strongly resembled her mother's.

The last of the Carson family was without any doubt the maverick. His name was Jerry. He was married to Joan, and between the two of them Charlie never could be sure of what was coming next. Charlie often wished he had been more like Jerry. If he could emulate his youngest son, he could go off to North Carolina with a carefree attitude that would help him overcome the grief that he had been feeling ever since his beloved wife had become ill. Charlie thought lovingly of the family that made him so proud. Under no circumstance did

Charlie want to jeopardize the reputation or the honor of his all-American family. But Charlie realized that the only way that he could help them would be to give them a very large amount of money as their legacy. Actually, they could all use a little bit of help monetarily. Unfortunately, Charlie was comfortable but he didn't have enough money to make a difference, especially when it would be divided by four. Charlie mused as he drove along the interstate, "Wouldn't it be fun to have the whole family over to my house for a party and to give each one a present. Let's see," thought Charlie, "each package would be the same size, the same shape—perhaps the size and shape of a thousand dollar bill. Of course, there would have to be hundreds of those bills in each package. How can I get several millions in a hurry? The only way that I know is to rob a bank."

With every mile that Charlie drove toward his favorite town in North Carolina his mind seem to rationalize his decision to leave his loving family in search of a more exciting life. Charlie had recently suffered a great loss when his wife died. The children attempted to encourage him to join one of them in their homes but that arrangement wasn't comfortable for anyone. Each time that Ethyl came into his mind the lonely, empty feeling seemed to permeate every cell of his body. This was followed by indecision and doubt in his ability to cope with the vacuum in which he found himself. The eldest son, Bill, suggested that Charlie spend a month with each family, but that wouldn't work. John advocated that Charlie move into a retirement home so that he wouldn't have any more chores such as yard work or cooking.

Charlie's thoughts questioned the numerous suggestions offered by everyone who had never been in this situation. "Why," he wondered, "should I leave my delightful little home? In all probability, I shall only last a few more years anyway. I'd much rather die here alone than in some home full of a lot of sick people. As long as I can move these old legs and as long as I'm capable of intelligent thought, I must maintain my independence."

As Charlie steered his car ever closer to the mountains of North Carolina, he questioned what the hell life was all about. If he lived several more years, would he be so bored that he would become a bitter old grouch, or could he develop some ambition or lifestyle that would permit him to go out in a blaze of glory?

Certainly, the thought of a sexual encounter didn't excite him, nor did the thought of traveling. Death was so inevitable, so final, and so damn close. He must act quickly, and he felt he should leave a great legacy to his entire family.

He was convinced that he needed to getaway from his family in order to be free from their recommendations. He was sure that under well-intended pressure, he would, sooner or later, yield to their wishes. The result would be that he'd become a burden and he would lose his autonomy.

He felt an urgency to spend a few weeks in his favorite part of the country. The Blue Ridge Mountains seemed to contain a magnetism that had drawn Charlie ever since he was a young boy. Charlie loved the mountains because they appeared so massive and dominant. The sweep of forests added to their mysticism and the forbidding rocks and jagged cliffs allowed one's eyes to pause in search of something—we know not what. The valleys were always the opposite. Their emerald green slopes extend invitations to everyone to come and play. The temptation is to wander aimlessly through the golden fields and over the white fences while the round-bellied cattle lay in the shade under a lone tree. The scene of homes and red barns stretched across the broad valley exuded peace and tranquillity while the snake-like brook wiggled its way past the foot of the rugged mountains. It appeared to be an area that would enhance family life.

# Two

The approach to Charlie's destination, Crystal Springs, North Carolina, is exquisitely beautiful. It is a very small town nestled in the mountains. It consists mainly of two roads that cross each other in the middle of town. The town can brag of one bank, about five stores, one restaurant, and two gas stations. In the center of town where the two roads intersect is a small park on one corner and a gas station on the other. There's a real estate building on the third corner. The road marked "17" goes north to the town of Diamond Cliffs past Lake Arrowhead. This lake is at least six miles long with the edge of several mountains tumbling into the deep green water. There are several waterfalls that feed into the lake toward the south end, and, at the north end, there's a large earthen dam that was built back in the 1940s by the TVA project. Over this earthen dam is a narrow two-lane road, plus a small bridge that's in serious need of repair.

The other road that crosses Route 17 in the town of Crystal Springs goes from east to west. This road is Route 46 and connects the town of Boulder Ridge on the east to the town of High Prairie on the west. Both of these routes are narrow, two-lane roads that wander through the mountains and valleys. These roads were originally foot trails probably made by Indians and, as a result, today they can be extremely dangerous to the careless driver.

Crystal Springs is located in a beautiful valley with heavily forested mountains mounting on every side. There are great quantities of rhododendrons and mountain laurel which are breathtakingly beautiful, particularly in the springtime when they're in full bloom. Prolific oak, maple, and locust trees crowd the slopes of the mountains.

Surrounding the town are pastures of bright green grass, shaded by huge old trees. Many farms extend up the valley between the ancient mountains. These farms vary from animal farms to those that are primarily planted with Christmas trees. It is truly a beautiful country area; there is no city life in this hilly paradise. Route 46 leaves Crystal Springs curling up the mountain through the farms and past many dirt roads, gradually gaining altitude until after about ten arduous miles it arrives in the much larger vacation town of High Prairie. This is a prosperous town full of tourists, mainly from Florida.

The mountain people are as unique as the area. Families originally came to these mountains and settled in the valleys. Each family claimed a valley as their own land and as the generations came along all the land in that particular valley was divided among each family's offspring. So each parcel was owned by a member of the same family. The only time that integration with other families took place was when a member of one family climbed the surrounding mountain and became involved with a member of another family in another valley. But more often competition grew between valleys, thus producing feuds such as the Martins and the Coys. The people in these green fertile valleys were industrious and hard working but unfortunately, due to the great distances that they must travel, they received little and in some cases no formal education. Their liberation came with the invention of the pick-up truck, for with it they could meet others, travel from the valley, and attend a common public school. Every young mountain dweller could drive a pickup on the dirt roads or in the back pastures. Learning to cope with country life concerned the farmers more than the book learning that was gained in schools.

Charlie became a little more alert as he approached the crossroads for at last he was arriving in his favorite town. He glanced at the bank as he came to the crossroads. A flood of thoughts again popped into his mind, mainly about robbing it.

When he approached Route 46, he knew that to get to his destination, a timeshare condominium, he must turn toward the east for a few miles on the way to Boulder Ridge. The road wandered to his condo, which overlooked part of the golf course called Mineral Mountain Golf Course. It was a gorgeous view with the mountains in the background, and beneath the porch lay the dark green fairways ending at a manicured green. It didn't take Charlie long to unload his car, mix a drink, and stroll on to the porch. He inhaled the invigorating mountain air, fresh as a mountain stream. Once again his thoughts reverted to the question: "Do I have the strength, or the brains, and, more importantly, do I have the guts to change the direction of my life? How do I accumulate a few million dollars in an extremely short time?"

"Maybe I could invest in the stock market. Hell, you'd have to be plain lucky to gain even a little bit."

"How about Texas, hit an oil well? No chance!"

"Maybe I could stick up a store. Nope! They wouldn't have enough money in the till."

"Hunt for gold? Ridiculous!"

"Invent something. Not possible!"

At last, Charlie concluded that his only alternative was to rob a bank. He half laughed at himself as he contemplated a picture of himself with a .45 pistol aimed at the tellers in a bank. To rob a bank is one thing, but the key is to getaway with it—otherwise it wouldn't help anyone. His children would probably be so ashamed of him that they would deny that they even knew him. Besides, it would be a disaster in the eleventh hour of his life, effectively making the previous eighty years worthless. Charlie came to one conclusion—that if he wanted millions in a hurry he must rob a bank and getaway with it.

# Three

The first project that Charlie needed to undertake was to observe the security that was available in and around the bank. The logic of robbing a bank in the mountainous areas seemed stronger because there were fewer cops or sheriffs around. Certainly, there were no cops patrolling the streets of Crystal Springs. According to the information that Charlie gathered, there was only one deputy to cover a wide area from High Prairie to Diamond Cliffs and from Crystal Springs to Boulder Ridge. This deputy's territory was so extensive that it could take forty-five minutes to one hour for him to answer an emergency call. In addition, there were only two main roads in or out of Crystal Springs. The rest of the roads consisted of dirt or gravel that disappeared into the surrounding forest and mountains. It was obvious to Charlie that he would stand a better chance here than any other place.

The townsfolk were good people who had rarely been exposed to the suspicion that commonly prevailed in larger cities. There weren't many robberies in these mountains, although once in a while a vacation house was robbed. In addition to this, the local residents were familiar with each other so it became almost impossible to commit a crime without being seen and identified. In fact, even Charlie was recognized by many of the locals for he had spent many summers in the area. This was probably one of Charlie's most serious problems. He must create a new image.

When Charlie was a boy, his father, a strict member of the Quaker religion, always felt that to be successful in life it was necessary to give the appearance of success. When Charlie went with his family to the Friends Chapel on Sunday to pray, everyone arrived in their best Sunday clothing. It was mandatory for Charlie to wear knee high socks with his best knickers, a jacket with a vest, and a very conservative tie. The image that the family wished to portray was one of being conservative, prosperous, and God-fearing. The senior Carson felt that one's physical appearance was worth more that seventy percent of one's entire image. His father, in spite of being a poor, honest, farmer, always felt that life began with hope. Hope of the future. Hope and desire that one could become successful "in any and all endeavors." And that these hopes then turned into dreams. The dreams were the direction used to mold the correct appearance. With every step, knowledge must grow in order to form a firm foundation that would support the appearance that the person was exhibiting. Appearance is the vehicle to success. Once the correct appearance was accepted by your fellow man, then you are what you wanted to be. So Charlie's father always preached to his children, "Appearance supported by knowledge shall make you a success." Charlie realized that if he wanted to be a mountain man with little or no identity then he must develop the correct image with clothing and a disguise.

One big question in Charlie's mind concerned his physical condition. Was he able to physically rob a bank, steal the money, and escape? After all, Charlie's body was succumbing to the eighty-year-old slump of the shoulders. Then, too, the shortness of his steps almost looked like the old-age shuffle. Even his shortness of breath put doubts in his mind. He knew that he must allow his brain to make up for his lack of brawn. But that brought up another question, "At eighty, is the brain even functioning correctly, when it allows him to attempt such a ridiculous venture?" Charlie's body shivered as he thought of the many obstacles that confronted him. The only thing that came to his mind was, "You're a crazy old man. But let's get to it anyway."

First, Charlie decided to analyze his own character, especially since he had never committed a felony in his life. In fact, he had never even thought about committing one. Charlie was a quiet, retiring personality who hated controversy. His wife had been the gregarious one, but he was always happier in the background solving problems and planning strategies. Next, he considered the fact that he would probably be under a lot of pressure from cops or vigilantes. He felt that at his age and experience that he could survive. Then too, he must consider his family. He could not even hint to them about his plans. They would undoubtedly be outraged with him just as he would be with them if they were acting this foolish. This meant that he could confer with no one! He questioned whether he should have a partner but the answer was always the same, a partner would be more trouble than he would be worth. Besides, whom could he trust? His conclusion was obvious—he couldn't tell a living soul. He had to do it alone!

Charlie walked around town. Crystal Springs seemed to be a perfect town to attempt his escapade. It had many dirt roads that could be used as an escape route. Charlie observed the bank from many directions. The front of the bank opened on the main road, Route 17, while the rear opened to a parking lot that was ringed with many huge maple trees where one could park a car quite inconspicuously. The exit from this parking area was superbly located, for it opened on to Route 46 to the west of the crossroads and then headed up the mountain toward High Prairie. This is the section of road where many dirt roads turn off toward the back country. In a matter of moments, one could have a choice of excellent escape routes.

Charlie then entered the bank through the back door, which was often used by those who parked in the parking lot. There was a long hall from the back door to the lobby with nothing to obstruct one's exit. As Charlie entered the lobby, he saw a surveillance camera mounted high in the corner so that it could easily cover the entire lobby. Next, he observed that there were only two tellers working at the same time. No one was sitting in the tiny front office. The drive-up window was located directly behind the teller's counter so that it was difficult to see into the bank from outside. Charlie's only chance would be to enter the bank from the back and announce that he had either a bomb or wave a pistol. Then, run around the counter, scoop up all the money in sight, while demanding that the tellers, who were all women, hand over all available cash. In a matter of a few moments, Charlie must run out the back door to speed off in his car toward the dirt roads into the back woods.

Charlie wanted to secure a relationship with the people in the bank so that he could come and go without really being noticed. So he introduced himself by asking to have change for two one-hundred dollar bills. Having accomplished his initial surveillance, he strolled out the front door, and then, turned into the real estate office where his friend from previous years sat, rocking in his favorite chair.

"Hi, Bobby Dee," Charlie called out.

Bobby Dee touched his hat while answering Charlie, "Doin' just fine, Charlie. I've been wondering when you were coming up here. Come on up." As Charlie mounted the steps up to the porch, Bobby Dee continued to talk. "We ain't got much business right now. Of course, we don't expect much. We have plenty of tourists in town but they're here to vacation not to buy property. The town is full to the brim, right now."

"Yeah, but it doesn't take too many people to fill this place," replied Charlie.

"We love all you people from the south coming up here for a vacation, but we don't cotton to the way that you're always in a hurry. You ain't goin' nowhere when you're on vacation, so why rush?" asked Bobby Dee.

"You're absolutely right. I bet that someone could shoot off a gun in this town and nobody'd even glance around," commented Charlie.

"That's true. One year we had old Malcolm from Mountain City ride right through this here town on his old gray horse."

"What's so unusual about that?"

"Well, sir," continued Bobby Dee, "he was dressed just like Lady Godiva. No one paid any attention to him until he tried to ride his old gray horse in the front door of the bank. Then, the manager of the bank grabbed the harness and led the old gray to the drive-thru. Well, a—course, the teller didn't say nothin', he just cashed the check and old Malcolm rode on out of town. I reckon that old Malcolm had had a little too much to drink, but I'll tell you this he put this metropolis on the map. I always wished we had named this town after him."

Charlie let out a loud laugh, then said, "I like the name of this town, Crystal Springs. It seems to fit the area so well, and I also like the fact that nobody seems to notice anything. It makes me feel like I can do most anything without being criticized."

"Where you staying this year?" asked Bobby Dee. "I'd like to have you over to my farm some evening when we're having an old fashion hoe-down."

"That's nice, I'd love to come, you name the date."

"Well, we have a get-together every once in a while 'cause this damned town is so quiet that we like to stir it up with some local music and some dancing. I'll let you know when," confirmed Bobby.

"I better run along right now for I got some shopping to do before I go back to my time-share over on the Mineral Mountain Golf Course. It's been good to see you again, Bobby," answered Charlie as he rose from the rocker to descend the steps.

It was at this point that Charlie realized that the possibility of putting on a disguise and wandering through town without being noticed was viable. This would be in harmony with his plan to rob the bank. He'd buy a wig, a mustache, a beard, and take out his upper teeth so that his face was distorted. Then he'd make an appearance in town just to see the reaction of some of the locals. As he walked around, he realized that to buy a wig, and several other things that he might use as a disguise it would be necessary for him to go to a larger town such as Mountain City. So the next day, he drove to the larger city where he purchased a shaggy wig, a small scanty beard that looked very realistic, and a mustache that accented his lack of upper teeth. Then on the way home, he stopped at a yard sale where he purchased some old work clothes that gave the entire disguise an authentic appearance. Back at the time-share, Charlie dressed in his complete disguise, stood in front of a full length mirror, and chuckled, for even he didn't recognize himself.

Now, it was time for Charlie to try out his disguise on other people. He drove to Crystal Springs, entered the local hardware store, and bought some batteries after asking one of the young female clerks whether he could return them if they didn't fit his battery-operated radio. There was no indication of suspicion by the clerk. Next, Charlie went to the grocery store, bought a few items with no one even looking or paying any special attention to him, for they had seen many mountain men dressed similarly to Charlie in their store. As he left the grocery store, he purchased the local newspaper, *The Crystal Springs Chronicle,* and then, sat on the bench near the front door. A man dressed as a farmer was sitting at the other end of the bench and within a matter of moments, the two men struck up a conversation.

"Oh, I come from down around Issaquah, out near the Cavender Meeting House," replied Charlie. "Do you know that area?"

"Yeah, but I ain't been there in years. That's pretty far off the highway ain't it?" questioned the farmer.

"Way out east," answered Charlie. Then the conversation continued for a short while until Charlie announced that he must move along. As he made his way back to his car, he felt very jubilant. Now, he was so confident that he purposely walked in front of Bobby Dee's Real Estate Office. He saluted Bobby Dee, who was sitting in his usual rocker. Bobby Dee's only response was a wave. This convinced Charlie that the disguise was a success. Now his plan was under way. During the next few days, he frequented almost every store in his disguise to establish his identity. Many of the townspeople now recognized him and waved as he walked by. It seemed easy to become accepted since there was such a small number of people. Even the bank personnel could be heard snickering when Charlie, dressed in his disguise, left the bank after asking directions to the nearest public laundromat.

Every day Charlie went to town and parked on Route 17 in the direction of Diamond Cliffs. Then he walked back to the intersection of 17 and 46 where he stood envisioning his best getaway route. The crossroads led in each direction to the only four roads out of town. His plans had to include an escape from these crossroads.

He tried. No luck on 17. He then tried Route 46 toward the south, but there was too much traffic. Next he headed toward High Prairie to the west. A small way outside of town there was a small dirt road that looked much like a private driveway. It turned abruptly off Route 46 to wind its way up into the mountains. It curved behind Lake Arrowhead into a valley where there were several farms. Charlie drove this country road for several miles past a pasture, where there were several overgrown farms with dilapidated barns. The road became narrower with each mile and the ruts became deeper as the road wound its way to the base of a mountain. Charlie was sure that this was the best country road for his escape route. He continued on the gravel road for another mile until he came to a lovely overlook. Here Charlie pulled his car on to the grassy area to see the view below him. What a sight it was! There below him was a beautiful pasture with healthy looking cattle languishing in the deep green grass. At the far end of the pasture was an old barn, half falling down on one end and with large double doors on the other. Charlie quickly realized that it would be difficult to spot his car from any direction. However, from his vantage point he could survey the entire pasture as well as have a clear view of the double doors of the barn. His thoughts confirmed the possibility of using this barn as his initial hiding spot for his stolen money.

Now is the time, he decided. He couldn't put it off. He slipped down the hill to make his way across the pastures. Then up the hill where the old barn stood. It was in dire need of repair. It looked as if a good hard push would make the old structure sort of lean for a moment and then gradually fall sideways, collapsing on the ground. But when Charlie entered the side door, he was amazed at the size of the main room, with huge timbers holding up a hay loft. It looked as though no one had used it recently for there was only a lot of dry hay scattered on the ground floor. As Charlie shuffled though the loose hay, it was obvious that this would make a good hiding place if he were to be successful in robbing the bank. As he kicked his way though the hay, his foot suddenly struck a metal hinge on the floor. Quickly, Charlie brushed away the loose hay with a well worn broom that he found in the corner. He discovered a trap door. Immediately, he assumed that this had been a storage cellar where the farmer had put his winter's supply of potatoes. When he lifted the door, he heard a lot of squeaking. It made him wonder if the squeaking came from the rusty hinges or from his old joints. The cellar was dark and damp with spider webs covering the entire opening. "This is a perfect hiding spot," was Charlie's only thought. He then covered it with hay and made his way back to his car.

As he drove away from his newly discovered valley, he could see someone walking along the dirt road. The man looked about his size with dirty clothes and a long beard. The man looked similar to Charlie when Charlie wore his disguise. The frayed hat covered his face so that only his unkempt mustache and beard was visible. The filthy jacket which was at least three sizes too big made him look like he had shoulders the size of a professional football player. Charlie eased his car next to the old man and rolled down the window, "Hi, can I give you a lift? I'm heading towards the crossroads." The man never answered but continued to hobble alongside the car. When Charlie saw the man's full face, he realized that this man was indeed a genuine mountain man. The man obviously had not washed in days. Once again Charlie asked, "I'm headed to town, can I give you a lift?" This time the old man backed off from the car as if he was afraid, then he made a slight bow with his head and mumbled, "Yas sur, thank you sur." He hobbled around the back of the car to open the front door. Before he entered he hesitated again, and pulled out a dirty rag to wiped off the seat.

Charlie smiled and said, "Please get in. What's your name? Do you live around here?" The old man looked across the pasture and pointed his hand, which was wrapped with a grimy handkerchief, toward the distant mountain.

Gradually, with prodding from Charlie, the old mountain man began to answer the questions. Charlie noticed that each answer contained a piece of a quotation taken from the great men of our country. When Charlie asked how long he had lived in these mountains the answer was, "Three score and seven years ago." Next Charlie asked why he wished to live alone in the woods, the old man replied, "I was conceived in liberty and I'm dedicated to be free and equal."

As Charlie pulled his car to a stop at the crossroads, he was aware that his passenger was exuding a foul body odor mixed with a breath of alcohol. Once again he asked the man's name and this time the old man showed that he was becoming more friendly because he answered with a strong proud voice. "Franklin Delano Roose."

Charlie restrained a laugh while asking, " Is there anything I can do for you?"

"No Sur! You don't have to ask what you can do for me, I should ask what can I do for you, (President Kennedy)."

Charlie retrieved a five dollar bill from his pocket and put it the old man's hand, "Don't drink it up, use it for food."

Franklin hesitated as he got out of the car, then said, "Thank you, Sur. But read my lips, this is not a new tax, (President Bush)."

# Four

Finally, Charlie had finished studying the layout of the old barn and the surrounding valley. He felt very confident. If he could escape the area around the bank and the crossroads, he could drive to the barn, open the doors, and hide the car in the barn until he could unload the money. This would give him plenty of time to bury the sacks of money under the hay or carry them up to the loft. Once that was accomplished, he could bide his time until he was positive that no one was in sight and then drive leisurely back to town.

As he turned up the hill on the route to his time-share. Charlie's first priority was to mix himself a drink, and plop down in the most comfortable chair on the porch in order to watch the golfers go by. At that moment, a man in the next apartment leaned over the railing and called, "Charlie, Charlie Carson, where the hell have you been? I expected you last week."

"Yeah, I know, I'm a little late this year. You look great, Jeff, how the hell have you been?"

"I'm sorry to hear about Ethyl, but I'm glad to see that you made it," answered Jeff Turner.

"I'm sorry to say that she had a tough time these past few months. I feel terrible that she's gone but at least she's out of pain now. I hope your wife is okay," replied Charlie. Jeff and Charlie had been friends for years. They had fished and played golf as often as their respective wives would allow them. They maintained respect for each other in spite of the fact that Jeff was relatively reserved about his life back in West Palm Beach. He did very little talking about his business except to say that times were not very prosperous at the moment. He was a great deal taller and a considerable number of years younger than Charlie. Yet there was a genuine feeling of comradeship between them. There had been times in the past that Charlie felt that he could trust Jeff as much as his own sons. But to trust him about his intentions of robbing the bank, that would be too much.

"Oh, yes, she's fine and just as picky as ever. How are all your kids and the grandkids? I'll bet you've got a mess of them now," continued Jeff. "I hope you brought your fishing equipment with you. How about trying the stream over near the waterfalls tomorrow?"

"Sounds great to me, I gotta show you the new fishing outfit that the kids gave me for Christmas. It's a whole new outfit for fly fishing. Can't wait, what time do you want to go tomorrow?"

"As early as possible—how about 6 A.M.?"

"Good, I'll be ready. We'll go in my car so your wife can have yours," replied Charlie.

"Okay."

Early the next morning, Charlie dressed in his new fishing garb with the hip boots that his youngest son had given him and met Jeff at the car. Both men wanted to talk continually for they held great respect for each other. There seemed to be a great deal to talk about for they hadn't seen each other for almost a year. Charlie immediately headed toward the waterfalls which were hidden deep in the woods. It was a very lonely place, but the brook was an ideal spot for fly fishing.

In no time flat, the two men had put on their boots and were wading in the fast-flowing, clear, cold water. Each man made several casts to no avail. At last, Jeff approached the subject of the death of Charlie's wife, Ethyl.

"Yeah," said Charlie, "the cancer gradually took over, no matter what we tried, until at last, all we could do was try to make her comfortable. It's a hell-of-a-way to go."

Jeff shook his head as if he felt every pain, then asked, "How did the kids take it?"

"The oldest, Bill, took it harder than the rest, 'cause he's a little more sentimental. Then after she died, we held a big meeting of the family to try to figure out how to live the rest of our lives without our guiding spirit. That was a tough period and it became obvious that I had become a fifth wheel in this family. Of course, I didn't want to become a burden to any of the children's immediate families. So I decided, over a lot of objections and advice, that I would remain in my little house at least for a year or so until something definitive showed up in my life."

"I think you're right; delay any decision for a time anyway. Then perhaps later on, you can discover a new life," agreed Jeff.

"You know, Jeff, you and I have nearly the same philosophy. We both want to keep everything in our lives as simple and direct as possible, and I always felt that life was at its best when it was serene and stable. Also, it would be outstanding if we had little or no illness nor any other serious problems. Consequently, I feel that it would be best for me to continue the same pattern of life as I have been living. You know that on my modest income plus my social security I can play my golf, visit my time-share, and watch this struggling world pass by until my final calling," Charlie's voice trailed off near the end of his sentence for his thoughts had silently reverted to the robbery and the legacy that he wanted to leave his family.

Jeff's voice jolted Charlie back to reality, "How's your daughter? She looks so much like your wife, Ethyl.

"Yeah," interrupted Charlie, although his mind had wandered to his new dilemma. The question was "Could Charlie go ahead with his plan?" He had been brought up to be honest and reliable. For his entire life he had followed the straight and narrow path, but now he would become a liar and a thief. Could he answer the question that Ethyl had always applied to difficult family decisions, "Can you live with your decision no matter what the outcome, and have you taken the high road?"

"No! No! Of course not!" exclaimed Charlie.

"What? What did you say, Charlie?" asked Jeff.

"Oh. I'm sorry, I was thinking about something else. I was thinking that I'm about ten years older than you are and I'm sure that your decision would be different if you were in my shoes. You see, my daughter, Susan, has been on my case for weeks. She insisted that I move into her small house with her husband and two kids. She kept it up until I had to yell at her that I was not staying with her family. I feel that my decision is the best for everyone."

Jeff was observing his old friend's character as he looked at Charlie across the stream. He was average height and weight and was very unimpressive at first appearance. But Jeff understood that although Charlie appeared to be a normal, reserved person, he was one who, over time as you got to know him, would dominate any occasion. His direction in life was along the straight and narrow path of truth and honesty, probably developed from his Quaker upbringing. His strength came from the compassion that he felt for others. He used to say from time to time, "Never mistake compassion or courtesy for weakness." Charlie had a knack for turning the other cheek until suddenly he reached his saturation point. Then without warning, he would explode. His wrath was so intense that one could believe that he was capable of doing physical harm to his opponent. Jeff also knew that some people believed that Charlie was vulnerable to severe pressure, but this always proved to be a fallacy. He would suddenly become a tenacious adversary.

Jeff liked Charlie as a good, polite, and loyal friend with an alert mind who usually showed no animosity toward anyone or anything. But no one realized how crafty Charlie could be. There were times when some friends would judge him as having old-age lethargy. "Far from it," thought Jeff, "Charlie is just planning his next maneuver."

Jeff once again turned his attention to his fishing.

"You're right, Charlie—Hey look! You got one! Pull 'em in!" yelled Jeff. "Don't lose him!"

Charlie's fishing pole bent like a rainbow. Charlie reeled in furiously every time the fish made a small jump. Gradually, Charlie moved a few steps closer to the fish in the cool mountain stream. In the meantime, Jeff was scrambling to reach the net so that he could help Charlie bring in the big sucker. Jeff quickly netted the wiggling fish. Then with dexterity, he slipped the hook from the mouth of the brook trout. It certainly was a fine specimen.

"That sure is a beauty. It's the best one that I've seen in a dog's age. If there's one here, there must be more," observed Jeff.

"It's funny, when you least expect it, it happens. I guess that's the way life is anyway," commented Charlie. "I wasn't paying any attention until you yelled. I'm sure I would have lost him otherwise."

The morning proceeded rapidly, measured only by the landing of a few more small trout, until at last, the two men agreed that they had better head for Johnny's Restaurant for lunch. As they drove over the back roads toward Johnny's, Charlie became conscious of the dense woods and the scarcity of people in this area. The dirt trails crisscrossed until one could easily get lost. It was obviously an area that no one traveled. The only thing that Charlie noticed was the sound of a waterfalls hidden somewhere behind the thick undergrowth. Immediately, Charlie recognized this as a logical place to permanently hide any loot that he might steal from the bank.

Soon, the two fishermen returned from the back woods to one of the main crossroads. As they circled into the parking lot behind the bank, an armored truck was in the process of collecting money from the bank. One guard sat in the driver's seat while the other brought sacks of money. Charlie made a quick excuse that he needed to get some money changed to smaller denominations. So he entered the bank while Jeff went on to the restaurant. This gave Charlie a good opportunity to see what procedure the guards were following. Moments after changing his large bills, Charlie exited the bank via the back door. His walk to Johnny's took him past his own parked car. It was filthy—even the license plate was nearly unreadable. Charlie commented out loud to himself, "I gotta get my car washed damn soon." But it was clear that Charlie's mind was focused on the exit from the bank.

After a sandwich and a coke at Johnny's, the two men headed back to the time-share. "I may be busy the next day or so because I've got a lot of people to see and a few chores to do, so I guess I won't be able to go fishing for a while," commented Charlie as he unloaded the fish from the trunk of his car.

The next day Charlie dressed in the clothes that he usually wore. He wished to walk through town as he would as if his wife was with him. He wanted to be seen as Charlie Carson not as Charlie in disguise. So he entered town and walked past the hardware store to the porch where Bobby Dee was rocking in his favorite chair.

"Hey, Bobby, what's happening?"

"Nothin'."

"You sit here every day, Bobby?"

"Yep. Love to watch people. Love to try to guess what they do for a livin'. I noticed several young men around here this week. There's one of 'em now. See, there he goes. See 'im? He's a great big kid, looks like a football player. I always wish I was big. I wouldn't be sittin' here if I was."

"What would you be doin'?"

"I think I would've been a lot more important than I am now. I could've played ball or boxed, or at least demanded a little more respect from my friends and neighbors."

"I guess we're all lookin' for respect," Charlie confirmed.

"Yep. Maybe I could've been a cop or a sheriff or somethin' like that. I could've investigated a lot of my friends who I think are a little bit on the crooked side. I think almost everyone has somethin' to hide."

"You're not including me in that, are you?" asked Charlie.

"Nah. You look like a regular guy. I'm talkin' about that young buck over there. He looks sort of suspicious. What would he want in this town? If he's lookin' to steal somethin' he better go to a bigger town than this. Last time we had a crime around here was about five or six years ago, when someone stole the sleepin' bags out of a window down at the camping and hiking store at the crossroads."

"How did they get in, break the windows?"

"Yep. I know who did it, too. I saw them stakin' out the place a couple of days before. I wondered what they were up to."

"Did the police catch 'em?"

"Nah. They got away."

"Didn't you tell the sheriff who did it?"

"Nah. Sheriff never asked me. But I knew those four sleepin' bags wound up in a store in High Prairie. But it's none of my business so I let it go."

"You mean, if they didn't ask you, you wouldn't tell 'em?"

"Oh, I'd tell if they robbed the hardware store or the market next door, maybe even the bank, 'cause the owners are all my friends. But the owner of that camping store is no friend of mine. He came over from Boulder Ridge way and I don't like him."

"Bobby Dee, I gotta go. Maybe I'll see you tomorrow. Don't sit there too long watching the people, you might see something that you don't want to see."

Charlie reviewed Bobby Dee's character as he stepped off the porch and headed to his car. On the one hand, he liked the real estate salesman who spent most of his time overseeing the town that Charlie loved, and Bobby's neighbors seemed to like him too. In addition, he was someone who was always available at a moment's notice to come to the aid of his fellow man.

# Five

At lunch time the next day, Charlie dressed himself in his complete disguise—wig, mustache, beard, no teeth, and old clothes that looked not only old but dirty too. He stood in front of a full-length mirror adjusting everything until he was convinced that no one, not even Bobby Dee, would know him. He planned to test the people in the area as to whether or not they would pay any attention to him.

This was beginning to be fun, and there was no doubt that he would need to practice his getaway. He drove into Crystal Springs and pulled his car into the parking lot behind the bank and relatively close to the armored truck. He parked the car in such a manner that it was facing the exit toward the crossroads, an easy spot from which he could make a fast getaway. He was still practicing. He got out of his car and approached the armored truck. There were no guards standing around the truck and the door to the front of the cab was open.

Charlie wandered close enough to see that there was no one in the driver's seat. Where was everyone? As he turned toward the bank he could see that the back door was ajar. It was such a hot day that Charlie figured that the bank clerks were trying to get some breeze through the building. An eerie feeling crept over his body like the hot flashes that his wife used to have. "Something must be wrong," he thought, "why would anyone leave the truck empty?"

Charlie made his way through the back entrance into the long hallway which connected to the front lobby of the bank. He could hear a voice that made his hair stand up on the back of his neck. Somebody was yelling commands to do something. He couldn't distinguish what was being said.

And then, female voices were capped by a scream of terror. Chills ran up and down Charlie's spine. Cautiously, Charlie poked his head into the lobby to witness a chaotic scene. The bank was being robbed! Suddenly, one of the men who was wearing a mask, wheeled around, and fired three shots over Charlie's head.

Charlie froze, his shoulders and arms raised as if to defend himself from a blow. His gasp seemed to make him hesitate at the entrance to the lobby.

A second robber with a stocking mask over his head was kneeling next to the driver of the truck and was in the process of tying him up. The truck's guard lay in a heap against the front door. He looked unconscious.

The third robber, who was wearing gloves in addition to his mask, had jumped over the teller's counter and was scooping up the loose money while stuffing it into large money bags. Charlie recognized these bags as those usually handled by the guards of the armored truck. This robber was a very large young man—six-foot-four or six-foot-five. He was ordering the women behind the counter to gather as much money as they could and fill the bags. The two women were obviously terrified and were acting exactly as they had been ordered.

As Charlie gave a cursory look at the entire scene, he attempted to back away when he heard the robber with the gun yelling, "Should I shoot him? Should I shoot him?"

"No!" screamed the one kneeling near the guard, "No one gets shot!"

Just then, the huge robber leaped over the counter holding several bags in his arms and headed toward the hallway where Charlie stood frozen.

Instinctively, Charlie grabbed one of the bags in an unconscious attempt to stop the robbery. The bag flew out of the robber's hands and the money flew through the lobby like large pieces of confetti. Bills of all denominations were floating throughout the bank.

Despite Charlie's fear, he chuckled audibly.

The fun ceased dramatically when the huge man turned and swung his mammoth fist at Charlie, catching him on the shoulder. The blow was so powerful that Charlie went sprawling across the highly waxed floor, until his head hit the leg of the desk.

Within moments, the three robbers grabbed several of the full money bags and headed out the rear door. Then, the robber with the AK-47 swung around toward the lobby and sprayed it with bullets. The surveillance camera broke into a thousand pieces, showering Charlie with glass.

Both tellers screamed in terror.

Charlie shook his head in order to clear the glass as well as the cobwebs. With difficulty, he struggled to his arthritic knees and then to his feet. He understood almost at once that he was the only one that was capable of doing anything in a hurry since the truck driver was tied and the lady tellers were in no condition to respond.

Instinctively, he readjusted his wig which had been knocked askew when he slid across the floor and sprinted through the back hall—as good a sprint as an old man could manage—out the door to his parked car. As he pulled the keys from his pocket, he could see the armored truck turning at the crossroads toward High Prairie. A car was leading the way followed by the armored truck. Charlie sped out of the parking lot and could hardly keep them in sight. As he gained speed, he noticed that the car and the truck suddenly turned off Route 46 on to a dirt road. "My God," he exclaimed out loud, "they turned onto the same road that I've been practicing on, the same get-away road!" Charlie picked up speed as he turned onto the gravel and followed as closely as he dared without being seen.

After two or three miles into the hinterland, Charlie realized that they were approaching the overlook where he had parked a few days before, the one that overlooked the valley with the old barn in the distance. Charlie pulled his car under a tree near the edge of the overlook and carefully crept to a position that allowed him to survey the barn more clearly. He could see the truck back up to the barn doors and disappear into the old barn. In the meantime, the third member of the gang had parked the car facing in a direction for a quick exit. Moments passed until at last the three men reappeared from the old rickety doors, allowing Charlie to realize that they had hidden the truck in the barn. He watched the three robbers enter the car, drive back on the dirt road, and head toward the mountain. It was obvious that they hadn't taken any of the money with them.

Charlie lay on the edge of the cliff considering what he should do next. He knew that the sheriff would set up road blocks on each of the major roads. As he bided his time, a light rain began to fall, making him uneasy and almost forcing him to act. It was obvious that nobody had followed the robbers and he calculated that the culprits would return for their loot the next day or sooner, after things cooled off a bit.

As Charlie rose to his feet, his feeling of loneliness grew, for he was the only one who knew where the money was hidden. His memory reverted back in time to when he was a youth in New England; the scene was very similar, for he had lived in a small stone cottage that was located at the mouth of a footpath that wandered though a thick forest ending near a very large pasture. He was lonely then, too, but the fresh smell of rain on the grass gave him a warm feeling. A wave of homesickness flowed over him for a moment. Then his thoughts were interrupted by the rain falling faster. He felt as if he had come full circle in his life but realized that there was no time to waste. He must make a quick decision. He had to act now!

He ran to his car and within moments he backed up to the rickety barn doors. With a great deal of effort, Charlie opened one door wide enough to squeeze into the barn. There stood the armored truck forlornly. Its doors hanging open and empty.

While sweeping his eyes around the inside of the barn, he could see there was no money in sight. The left side of the barn had deteriorated so badly that the sky and the rain were entering the barn as if the roof had blown off. On the right side of the barn were scattered piles of loose hay just as he had seen when he was there before. Part of the hay looked as if someone had been sleeping there in the past. Immediately, Charlie inspected the truck to make sure that it was truly empty. Then he kicked through the hay in the corner of the building. Every step he took made him wonder where the robbers had hidden the money. Just as he was becoming frustrated, his toe struck one of the heavy canvas bags. Quickly, he scraped away the dusty hay while pulling out several other bags. They were all full of money! Now what should he do?

Charlie's mind raced. He could go in any number of directions. He could take the money, he could call the police, he might bury it someplace here in the barn, he might even bury it in the mountains, he might run to the time-share or even to Florida. Nothing sounded very good to him, but whatever he was going to do, he had to do it fast. Working quickly, he began to load the bags of money into the trunk of his car.

Then he peeked out the double doors to see if anyone was coming. He could feel the rain coming harder and the sky looked even more ominous. There was no one around and so he hurried back to his car to finish loading the bags into the trunk. Occasionally, he stopped to rip open a bag with his pen knife. Each bag was filled with packets of money. Cash! Cash! Cash! That's all he saw.

Now he must get out, but first, he should change his clothes. He would have a better chance of being ignored if he looked like himself instead of a derelict. So off came the beard, then the wig, and of course, at last, he put his teeth back in his mouth. He quickly slipped into his better clothing. Now he felt more normal. Charlie threw his disguise into the trunk of the car with the bags of money, then looked at his watch. This scenario had taken a great deal of time, in fact, much more than he realized. Surely, by now, the roadblocks must have been set up on every road out of Crystal Springs. How could he get by them? His only way home to the time-share would be on the main Route 46 back to the crossroads. He drove his car along the dirt road until he reached the edge of 46. Cautiously, he nosed his car beyond the trees so that he could see to his right. There, up near Wildcat Cliffs, the police had set up a roadblock. It was obvious that they were stopping all traffic that was headed towards High Prairie, but none that was headed towards Crystal Springs and the crossroads. Now Charlie realized that he had no choice, he must go to the crossroads.

Two cars heading for the crossroads pulled past the front of his car, so Charlie swung in behind them as they circled down the mountain. All three passed the intersection without incident, then headed up the hill toward Mineral City. Charlie looked towards the bank as they pulled through town. There seemed to be people everywhere, especially in the parking lot behind the bank. By now, the rain was falling in an old-fashioned downpour. Charlie could see lots of police and deputy sheriffs maintaining the road block at the top of the hill on the way out of town. Between the rain and the creeping darkness, it was difficult to see all of the activity going on at the road block.

As Charlie approached the road block, his heart was in his throat but he knew he must gamble on the rain, on his appearance, and on the quickening darkness to help him past his last obstacle. When he arrived one car from the road block, he saw that the deputies were opening some of the car trunks. "Oh, shit, they're searching the trunks," he muttered to himself as he fought back a wave of nausea. He tried desperately to think of something to say so that they would allow him through, but no wise thoughts came to mind. Charlie rolled the window down, expecting to have a sheriff yell for him to get out of his car, when he heard a voice saying, "Is that you, Charlie?"

"Yeah," he answered, "Who's asking? I can't see you in the dark."

"It's me, Bobby Dee."

"What are you doing out here in the rain, Bobby? Are you part of this road block?"

"Yep," replied Bobby. Then he turned toward the other members of the road block and called out, "Let this one go through, he's a friend of mine. We gotta get this traffic outta here, it's beginning to pile up." Then turning back to Charlie he said, "Hey, Charlie, move along, I'll see you tomorrow, we got a lot to talk about now."

Charlie's feelings suddenly changed from desperation to euphoria. His grip on the steering wheel softened but he pressed his foot on the accelerator too hard, causing the car to lurch forward. The deputies jumped back, angrily waving him through.

Visibly shaken, Charlie drove to his time-share. He knew he couldn't unload his car right away for fear someone might see him carrying bags of money into the condo. Besides, he couldn't leave the bags inside the condo because the maids would come to clean the next day.

After fumbling with the key at the front door, he finally managed to unlock it, then stumbled past the fireplace and finally flopped into his favorite chair. He immediately clicked on the local TV station. The news was solely concentrating on the magnitude of the robbery in Crystal Springs.

The young female commentator was classifying the robbery as world class. Then she continued to explain how three professional robbers had entered the bank with automatic weapons and terrorized the employees. She told how the armored truck guards had been injured and how an old mountain man had been knocked down when the robbers ran out of the bank. She then reported that part of the tape used in the surveillance camera had shown that the three thugs were wearing ski masks and the tape showed a very brief picture of an old man.

In an interview, the bank teller confirmed that an old man had gotten in the way of the robbers and that he was hit by one of the robbers, sending him sprawling across the floor. "It looked like the old man was wearing a wig because his hairpiece was off to one side of his head," the teller added.

The news reporter asked the clerk if she could interview the old man.

"I don't know where he is," answered the teller. "Hey, Martha, where's that old man?"

"I don't know. No one's seen him since he went sailing into a desk. Even the sheriff is looking for him," answered Martha.

# Six

As Charlie tried to relax in his favorite chair, he was worried that many of the townspeople were looking at the same tape on TV that he was watching. In all probability, Charlie must assume that someone would make a connection between the mountain man and the old tourist from Florida.

A review of his predicament did not seem to afford him any new answers. If he kept the money, Charlie reasoned, his life and his children's lives would be changed. If he ran with it, he would be caught. If he gave it back, he would have to tell the police that he had stolen it from the crooks in order to prevent them from getting away with it. But that wouldn't be logical because he didn't return it immediately. Then again, Charlie tried to approach the problem from a different angle. Why should he give it back? This was one chance in a million, or maybe ten million, that a person would stumble on a fortune and no one would know anything about it. He felt that most of his friends wouldn't give the money back either. This was Charlie's big chance.

Unexpectedly, Charlie suddenly heard his wife as clearly as if she was in the room, "Can you live with this decision, Charlie? Have you taken the high road? Are you going to hurt anyone?"

"No! Dammit! No!" yelled Charlie. "I've given up everything else in my life—my health, my wife, my youth, my children are gone—there's not much left. So this is my last chance to have millions, I won't give that up. It's a large enough amount to be worth the risk."

Again on the eleven o'clock news, Charlie watched the report. The tape clearly showed him enter the bank through the hallway. Charlie noticed immediately that the tape showed his wig slightly askew and that one of the deputy sheriffs had referred to him as the "old geezer." It was apparent to Charlie that from then on everyone referred to the old mountain man as the "old geezer." Even the reporters, once again, described how the "old geezer" was knocked to the floor by the very large young robber. Since there was no knowledge of his whereabouts, a plea by the police was made, requesting that the "old geezer" turn himself in for questioning. The reporter stated that he was not a suspect but it was possible that he might help the investigation.

As the night dragged on, Charlie investigated every avenue he could think of and still keep the money. His most promising plan seemed to revolve around temporarily hiding the money until the heat was off. Then he would have to find a way to give the money to his children. They would be very suspicious of any story that he might tell them. Especially the second son, who was extremely honest. Maybe if Charlie bought some lottery tickets, he could tell his children he had won the grand prize. None of his kids ever look at any lottery in any state other than Florida. By giving them a large amount of money when he arrived home, he might be able to persuade them to accept his word about the lottery. Perhaps he could get one of those fake newspapers with headlines saying that he had won the lottery. Charlie felt that this was his best chance.

As the evening progressed his head began to ache, so Charlie slipped into bed, and slept fitfully. Morning brought sunshine and a new impetus to Charlie's desire to solve his problems. He quickly dressed in his own clothes. He shaved, combed his hair, and admired that his teeth seemed to fill out the hollow look of his face. Having approved of his present appearance, he drove into town to see the kind of excitement that the townsfolk were experiencing after yesterday's robbery.

The town never looked busier, and Charlie had to drive around several times in order to find a parking space. He was ashamed of his car. He never could remember it being as dirty as it was now. The mud was so thick that you might have trouble seeing through the windows.

Charlie wandered through the small town. First, he went to the stores, which were busier than he had ever seen them. Then he circled around toward the bank. News reporters were interviewing several local townspeople and deputies were controlling the mob of people that were trying to peek into the scene of the crime. Everyone seemed to be talking at the same time and pointing first at the bank, then at the get-away route toward the crossroads. Workmen were laying cable and various electrical wires to trucks that were marked News TV and Radio. Charlie stepped deftly over the cables toward the marketplace, dodging the police that had been brought in from some of the surrounding towns. It was obvious that everyone was expressing their theory about what happened and how it took place.

As Charlie approached the real estate office, he could see Bobby Dee sitting in his special rocking chair, watching all the activities going on in the town. "Hey, Charlie, come on up here on the porch," called Bobby Dee, "sit with me a spell. I'm so excited about this whole affair."

Charlie climbed up the steps, slipped into the extra rocking chair next to Bobby, and let out a sigh of relief.

"You know, Charlie, I surely hate to say this but I think this is the best thing that ever happened to Crystal Springs. This will certainly put us on the map. There's talk that the governor is going to come here tomorrow to oversee the police," said Bobby Dee.

"Perhaps," answered Charlie, "I appreciate your getting me through the roadblock last night. Have they got any new clues this morning? It seems a shame the cops haven't found the punks or skunks, whatever you want to call them."

"The sheriff has a few leads but nothing very positive. He told me last night that he has to question everyone from around the bank—tellers, merchants, customers, and even the old mountain man. You know who I mean, the one who was knocked down during the robbery. Everyone's lookin' for him, but he's vanished. The sheriff thinks the old man might have followed the crooks out of the area."

"What about the crooks?" questioned Charlie. "I'm sure by this time they've split up the money and they're out of the area. They're probably half way across the country—maybe in Canada or Mexico. How much money did they get, anyway? It looks to me like they knew exactly when to hit the bank so the truck would be there at the same time. It looks to me like they had done a lot of planning to getaway so cleanly."

"Yep," replied Bobby Dee. "Must have been, especially since no one's found the truck or any other clue. They don't even know which way they went when they got to the crossroads. They probably drove over the mountains last night through the back woods and by now they're in Tennessee or Kentucky."

Bobby Dee paused to watch a heavy-set young man walk past the edge of Bobby Dee's porch then cross the street toward Johnny's Restaurant. "Boy, I wish I was that guy's age. I'd go after these robbers myself, especially if they offered a reward. Sheriff Macklin said that there will probably be a reward since the money that was stolen was in the millions."

"I understand that tomorrow the sheriff's going to appoint a bunch of young men from this area as deputies to scour these back woods in hopes of finding the truck or the money or some indication of what happened. What would you do if you were in charge, Charlie?"

"How the hell do I know? I don't believe those crooks are still in this area. They've flown the coop. They probably took the whole kit and caboodle and fled to Arizona or Idaho. Who knows, maybe they've even gone overseas."

"Boy, that dates you, Charlie. I haven't heard kit and caboodle since my grandfather was alive. How old are you anyway? Seventy-five? Eighty? Whatever, you still look younger than that "old geezer" that got hit in the bank.

"I hope so. He looked like he was pushing ninety to me."

"Sheriff Macklin's a little suspicious of him," replied Bobby. "The sheriff told me this morning the police are sure the "old geezer" was wearing a wig. So supposin' he was wearin' a fake beard too. What's he hiding? Maybe he's hiding from somebody or maybe he's involved with the robbers."

"Nah, I don't believe that," said Charlie. "I think we're jumping to conclusions. Bobby, have you ever seen this many people in Crystal Springs? This town has become a city overnight."

Occasionally, as Charlie and Bobby Dee sat there in their rocking chairs, someone from the crowd would stop to ask directions or where the police station was. But most times the question was, "Have they caught anyone, yet?"

Bobby Dee seemed to know a lot of the people who passed his porch. He either waved or yelled "Hello" to them, and many would stop to chat for a while. When Bobby Dee began questioning Charlie about his past, apparently to become more friendly, a young man dressed in the typical clothing of the local residents, dungarees, and a plaid flannel shirt interrupted Bobby Dee to ask him where the police had set up their headquarters.

"Sheriff told me that they're taking over the Trolley Station Restaurant on Route 46 across from Blue's lumber yard. I wouldn't go near there today if I were you, too many cops, and I hear the FBI may be comin' in today or tomorrow. I suppose they'll set up in the same place."

Abruptly, Bobby Dee began talking about the current problems of the local merchants. "You know, Charlie, all the storekeepers are really happy with the publicity we're getting from this robbery, because the people are coming in droves and they are buying everything in sight. Johnny's Restaurant has had lines out the door all day long and the owner of the Exxon gas station told me a few minutes ago that he called the supplier to make an extra run so he wouldn't run out of gas over the weekend."

"Well, maybe there is some good coming out of this after all. Bobby, what would you do with all that money?" asked Charlie, "Would you run? Or would you try to hide the cash somewhere around here?"

"I think I'd just bury the bags and wait for the whole thing to cool off. No one could find my hiding spots. They'd have to dig up the whole side of the mountain. There are spots out here that no human has ever set a foot on. So they wouldn't have a chance in hell of finding them."

"I suppose you're right, but someone might see you when you went to hide the bags. It would be pretty risky, I'm sure."

"It's easy to see that you're not from around here," Bobby Dee said. "There are so many back roads, especially through some of the farms in the back hills and valleys, that most anyone could drive up to the edge of the woods and pick any spot with no one the wiser."

"You make it sound so easy, but I'm sure it wouldn't be that easy for someone my age or for someone who didn't know the area," said Charlie.

"You're right about that—look who's coming this way, it's Sheriff Macklin. He'll take a half hour to get here. Look at all the folks trying to talk to him."

"Gee, I'm sorry," Charlie broke in, "I've gotta go. In fact, I'm late now. I've got an appointment at the medical center, I better hurry along. I'll stop in tomorrow, Bobby Dee. See ya."

"Bye, bye, old man," Bobby kidded Charlie.

Skillfully, Charlie allowed himself to be absorbed into the crowd of people on the street and soon he had disappeared from Bobby's view.

Bobby Dee's attention was drawn away when the sheriff appeared on the steps of Bobby's porch.

"Hi, Bobby Dee."

"Hi, Sheriff, How you doin'? Gettin' anywhere with this whole thing?"

"I don't know. Sometimes I think I am, then sometimes I think that this whole robbery didn't turn out the way the crooks planned it. I have the feeling that something went wrong, but I can't put my finger on it yet."

"What do you mean?" asked Bobby.

"Well, if these kids were the only ones stealing the money, then what the hell was that "old geezer" doing in the middle of the whole thing? And then, too, we feel sure he followed the truck when the crooks left. He was the only one in a position to see which way the truck went. Where was his car all that time? Martha, one of the tellers in the bank, told me that the "old geezer" had a dirty old Toyota, but nobody has seen him or the car today."

At this point Bobby Dee thought out loud, just loud enough for the sheriff to hear, "Charlie's Toyota is dirty as hell!"

# Seven

When you leave Crystal Springs and drive west for about ten miles, you arrive in the beautiful tourist town of High Prairie. There are more Florida license plates in this town than can be found in many of the counties in Florida. The pharmacy on main street in High Prairie was jammed with people sitting at the counter eating an early lunch. Charlie made his way to the rear of the store and stood behind one of the stools at the counter. Within seconds, one of the customers wiped his mouth of food, dropped fifty cents on the counter, and relinquished the stool to Charlie. Conversations were so prevalent around the lunch counter that the entire store was immersed in a rumbling drone. The main topics were the same here as they were in Crystal Springs. Who robbed the bank? Where did the thieves go? What happened to the "old geezer"? Where's the money now?

Charlie felt sweat trickle down his back. He realized that he really didn't want to talk or even think about it anymore, but there was no escaping it in these mountains. He began to feel as if he was being pressured by everyone. He decided to finish his coffee, go to the gas station to buy the lotto tickets, and then he felt that he had better open a bank account in the High Prairie bank so that he could have a convenient place to change larger bills into smaller ones, and also he could have a bank to make small deposits from which he could write local checks. At this point Charlie's reasoning wasn't very clear, but he realized that he needed a new image, so he transferred a couple of thousand dollars from his Florida account to a new account in High Prairie.

As he walked out of the bank, he felt that this was a good time to test the passing of some of the cash from the theft. He pulled his car down the back road near Wick's Restaurant. There he opened the trunk, reached into the bag of money and pulled out a couple of packets. Quickly, he scanned the packets to be sure that the money was not in rotation and that he could not find any other markings. Then he took five hundred dollars and went back to the bank to add to his new account.

Charlie went to the window and deposited the cash. The woman teller greeted him pleasantly, "Good afternoon, Mr. Carson. I just processed your new account. My name is Mrs. Botts and I welcome you to our bank." Charlie saw that she paid no particular attention to the money that he deposited. His concentration faulted momentarily, as he was taken by the pleasant attitude of the bank clerk. Her smile was captivating and her voice so soothing that Charlie forgot about the purpose of his opening an account. He felt that she was not as old as he but that she had a maturity that instilled assurance and cheerfulness. Her appearance was wonderful, with her gray hair and her exquisite profile. Charlie felt that this was one lady that he would like to know. He immediately felt relief and commented on the fact that he was glad the robbers hadn't hit this bank. He watched Mrs. Botts handling the bills as she stacked them in her money drawer.

"We've never had a robbery here that I know of," said Mrs. Botts

Charlie thanked her and hesitated before leaving, until he realized that to stay any longer would be uncomfortable for them both, so he left with a warm feeling and a belief that the money was unmarked. As a matter of fact, it was the same feeling that Charlie had when he learned that he had passed his final exams. Having opened his new account and passed some of the money, he then purchased a hundred dollars worth of lotto tickets and took off for his time-share in Mineral City. He was sure that the most important task now was to find a really safe place to hide all that money.

At first, he thought that it would be easy to hide the money, but as time went on, he came to the conclusion that it was not a simple maneuver. First, he considered hiding it in an old tree, but he knew that wouldn't be big enough. Next he thought of hiding the money in a cave or under some rocks. How about near a waterfall, like the one on the thirteenth hole on the golf course? But nothing seemed to be very promising. His thoughts reverted to the idea of a waterfall. That seemed much more appealing to him, especially since he knew of one that was hidden in the heavy woods. He remembered hearing the roar of the water when he was fishing with Jeff the other morning. He began to feel more comfortable with the location, for he knew that there was only an old lumber trail near it, and he also knew that there were very few people who ever went into that part of the woods. In order to get there, one had to travel down a wet path then through a thickly wooded area before arriving at a small stream. Then you'd have to cross the stream on a fallen log in order to go down a very slippery path, until one reached a narrow shore of a pond where the falls emptied. The waterfalls were approximately fifteen feet high and the water splashed on many rocks at the bottom. This would be the best spot possible, but he knew he must put the bags of money in something that would stay dry. Then he could bury them so that there would be little or no chance of anyone discovering them. The first thing that came to his mind was to put the bags in an ice cooler that one uses on picnics. He knew he must buy several of them to protect so many bags. He planned to keep the money there until he could figure a way to get the money to his kids in Florida. He might use the cold storage bin in the floor of the barn that he found the last time he was there. But when the armored truck was found by the police, they would most certainly search the rest of the barn and find the cold storage area. So that place wouldn't be viable.

As he drove from High Prairie toward his time-share, he came to the spot where the deputies had set up their road block the day before. There were lots of cars ahead of him. They seemed to be going in and out of the driveway that he'd used as his getaway route.

"What's goin' on?" he called to the police who was directing traffic. "Is this another road block?" His stomach did a couple of flips and for a moment he thought that they would make him open his trunk.

"Just keep the road open for the fire trucks," answered the cop, "Come on, keep movin'. They found the armored truck, down that way."

Quickly, Charlie swung his car into the dirt driveway and headed toward the old barn where he knew the robbers had hidden the armored truck. As he pulled onto the overlook, he could see many people and several fire trucks scurrying around the old barn. The barn was ablaze! The flames leaped high into the air as the entire barn was engulfed. Charlie leaned over toward an older man standing next to him to ask, "What's goin' on? Who started the fire?"

"Don't know who done it, but they say that the armored truck was inside. That's the old Owen's barn. Looks like it's going to collapse now," answered the old farmer.

It looked like everyone for twenty miles around had arrived in the valley. There were volunteer firemen running hoses from the small ponds up to the fire and they were pumping as much water as they could onto the barn. The mud around the barn was as thick as snow in the middle of winter. It was apparent that the barn could not be saved, but the sheriff wanted to save as much as possible for evidence. On one end of the barn the deputies were already looking through the residue by the time Charlie walked down through the pasture. He would stop off and on to talk to one of the young men about the fire. No one knew anything, and no one seemed to understand why the crooks had set fire to the truck and barn.

"Isn't it crazy that the robbers would take the money from the truck, then set it on fire?" questioned one of the volunteers. "You'd think they'd just take the money and run as fast as they could."

At this time, Sheriff Macklin came up to the chief of the fireman. "Hey Mac, see if there is any residue in the back of the truck. I want to know whether the crooks took the bags with them. And also I want a detail of men to search for tire tracks around this barn. I know it rained after the robbery but someone came up here today after the rain. I don't think the crooks unloaded the truck last night, I think they came back this morning to get the money. What do you think, Mac?"

"Yeah, I think you're right, 'cause when I got here I could only see one set of tire tracks and they looked like they came from a pick-up. Now with all this mud you couldn't be sure of anything. Of course, the one set of footprints that I saw have been wiped out by the spray from the hoses. Makes me think there was only one man here this morning," replied Mac.

"I'm sure that we'd see a lot of footprints going in and out if they loaded the pick-up today. And you said that the footprint was a much larger size than yours," answered the sheriff.

"Right, and we know that all three crooks were very large men, at least six-three or six-four. All the witnesses verified that. Then I'd like to know why they came back here if they took the money last night. Did one man come back here alone just to set the fire?" questioned the fire Chief.

"Not likely," commented the sheriff. "Is it possible that someone else found the money and removed it before the original crooks came back to get it?"

That was enough for Charlie to hear; he could anticipate the next logical conclusions that the two men would make, so he immediately headed back though the pasture to his car. By the time he drove over the dirt roads back to Route 46, he was aware of a red pick-up truck parked on the side of the road. Charlie settled back in his driver's seat with a sigh of relief, but upon looking in the rearview mirror, he noticed that the red truck pulled out on to the road. It dawned on him that he had seen that same truck somewhere in Crystal Springs. It was the blond kid who was driving. The one that Bobby Dee was envying because of his size. Anxiously, Charlie increased his speed after he drove through the crossroads, but when he sped up so did the truck. He deliberately increased his speed then decreased it only to find that the red pick-up did the same. This annoyed Charlie greatly. He felt that he could not head for his time-share. That guy was not just tailgating him for the fun of it; there must be another reason.

As Charlie passed Johnny's Restaurant, he pressed his foot to the accelerator until he was speeding at sixty-five miles an hour on these narrow, windy roads. He didn't dare go any faster. It was too dangerous. He was hopeful that he could get to the hotel where there were a lot of people.

As he approached the entrance to the hotel, he glanced in the rearview mirror and noticed that the truck was dropping back until at last it turned off. Charlie pulled into a parking lot where he parked for an extended length of time, trying to calm himself down.

It seemed that there was pressure on him all the time. "What the hell did that son-of-a-bitch want with me? Maybe he recognized my car. Who the hell can I tell about this?" were a few of the many questions that this truck raised in Charlie's mind. But this was just another problem for Charlie, because he had come to a point where he must decide how to handle several major problems. Now, he began to work out the details of his plans. First, he must hide the money somewhere near the waterfalls. In order to do that, he must buy several picnic ice chests and a shovel to enable him to bury the chests and an ax or a machete to clear the brush. Next, he needed to explore the waterfall's area for a likely spot. After he had the chests buried, he must then concentrate on a plan that would include telling his children that he had won the lotto. This would be the tricky part because he would have to make it a plausible and believable story. He was convinced that he could hold a party and give out identical presents to each one of his children and the same amount to the grandchildren. Cash, packets of cash!

He might as well make the gifts really big, because after all, that is what he had the most of now. Each year from then on, he would give away as much as he could—tax free! Another problem that he felt he could solve was the question of staying up on all the breaking news. Therefore, his best channel of information would be through Bobby Dee. He must cultivate a close relationship with him. Also, he felt that if he wished to disappear for a day or so that he could invite Jeff to go fishing and therefore, Jeff might become a good alibi.

As he continued to review all of his options, he came to one conclusion that had evaded him ever since this adventure began. It was a truth that he had known years ago but had put out of his mind as if it were nothing. He suddenly realized that there is no particular point in being a millionaire unless it could be shared with someone, or at least have the freedom of spending large quantities of money on loved ones. To sit counting one's gold like Midas was idiotic. He had learned with the death of his beloved wife that life rarely meant anything unless it could be enjoyed with a second party. He wanted to talk about the things that had happened to him.

When he arrived at his condo, his first thought was to call his unmarried son. He decided to tell him about the events of the last few days and to ask him to come up to help.

"Hello, Johnny? This is Dad." But before Charlie could add another word, Johnny interrupted.

"Now Dad, Susan is here and we have decided that we don't want you up there all alone. I'm sure you're going to get into too much trouble. So we want you to come home right away."

"No," answered Charlie, "not now, I'm just beginning to have fun. Let me tell you what has happened."

But at this moment, Susan interrupted from an extension phone, "Dad, now please come home at once. We've found a good place for you to live here near us. We can't take care of you when you're so far away."

His two children kept up a steady badgering, until at last, Charlie's usual reaction took hold. He could never take pressure to do exactly what suited other people. "Now listen to me, dammit. I'm not coming home now and I planned to tell you about my escapades but now, you'll have to wait until later."

But once again, Susan interrupted. This time, Charlie's blood pressure jumped about fifty points. "Listen, I'm not coming home now and believe me, sometimes, you two are a pain in the butt! I'm fine and I'll call you sometime next week. Goodbye."

Charlie hung up with a guilty feeling about losing his temper.

# Eight

Early the next morning, Charlie drove his dirty old car toward Boulder Ridge with all of the stolen money still in the trunk and plenty of small bills in his pockets.

His shopping trip to the larger city was successful. He stacked the ice chests inside each other and with a new machete and shovel he headed back to the lumber trail near the Silver Run Falls. Cautiously, he maneuvered his car through the curvy dirt roads, always getting nearer to the hidden falls. At last, he had approached as close as was possible. Now, he knew that he had his work cut out for him. He spent most of the rest of the day working, all alone. He carted the money bags out of the trunk of his car into the woods, across a huge log that had fallen across the narrow stream, then up a slippery hill, and finally, to a large hole that he had dug into the bank near the side of the waterfall. It took several trips to carry the bags, then many more trips to carry the ice chests. By the time he had dug the hole and carried all of the chests and bags, he was hot and tired, especially for an old man. He meticulously put the bags of money into the chests, then sealed them with tape to keep them dry, and at last he buried them in the hole with plenty of brush and leaves thrown over them. He felt the chances were very slim that anyone could find them. Finally, Charlie made his way back to his car, stopping only to wash his face and hands in the fast-flowing stream. As he was walking down the dirt road carrying his shovel and ax, a voice called out, "Mr. Carson! Hello! That is you, isn't it, Mr. Carson?"

Charlie's face flushed with fear as he turned to see a woman waving at him. She was a little distance away so he couldn't recognize her immediately. Although the dog at her heels was very large, he looked friendly, with his tail wagging continuously. All at once, it dawned on Charlie that he had seen this lady at the High Prairie Bank. The one that he had admired and wished he could know socially.

"Yes, I'm Charlie Carson, aren't you Mrs. Botts from the bank?" questioned Charlie.

"Yes, of course, whatever are you doing out here on this old logging trail?" she asked.

Charlie had to think quickly, for he had been caught off guard, "You wouldn't believe it, but I came out here to steal a couple of small holly trees that I can plant near my condo. Planting trees at my age! I'm afraid I won't live long enough to see them grow very tall," he commented, with a chuckle in his voice.

"Mr. Carson, you're not that old. In fact, I believe that you're only a little older than I am. I'll bet those trees will grow to ten feet tall in the next couple of years. I love to see people planting things. I think we should all do more of that. Whew," she added as she wiped her hand across her forehead, "it sure is hot today."

"Sure is. I tried to cool off down at that little stream in the woods, but I'm still too hot to be wandering around out here in the sun. I figure I'd better find a shady spot to rest in for a while," Charlie answered as he mopped his brow with a handkerchief.

"Better than that," observed Joanne Botts. "Why don't you come to my house and have a coke? I live just about a quarter of a mile around that bend in the road. We can sit on the porch where there is usually a cool breeze."

Charlie hesitated, but since he was feeling very hot and tired, agreed to accept the invitation. The dog seemed to anticipate the change in direction and led the couple back to Joanne's house.

The house was a small cottage with two bedrooms, a living room, and a kitchen, but the most outstanding part of the house was the porch, which wrapped around three sides of the house. It was obvious that Joanne was a woman who took good care of everything she owned, for the house was neat and well kept. The view from the porch did not encompass the mountains, but was directed to a lovely babbling brook that snaked its way through her front yard. Charlie sat in a rocker admiring the peaceful setting as Joanne went to get a tray of cold cokes with ice.

"Oh boy, that's great," said Charlie.

"Yes, I love a coke in the afternoon. It seems to give me a lift. Even though it's close to dinner, it doesn't matter to me."

"Yep, I can drink a coke any time," commented Charlie. "Tell me, how'd you come to settle here in these mountains?"

"Oh, about six years ago, my husband and I decided to retire here in the mountains. He retired from an engineering firm in Ohio. When we moved down here he developed heart trouble and he died two years ago."

"I'm sorry to hear that. I had a quadruple bypass a couple of years ago myself. Ever since then I get kind of tired and out of breath. But actually, I'm in pretty good shape for my age. Nowadays, I worry about my sons more than myself. They're at that dangerous age—fifty to sixty."

"How many children do you have?"

"Three sons and a daughter," answered Charlie.

"I have a daughter too. She called me last night to ask me about that robbery in Crystal Springs. I guess the national newspapers have picked up on it now. Have you heard anything new today?"

"Yes," said Charlie. "Yesterday, as I traveled from High Prairie to my time-share in Mineral City, I noticed a lot of cars on Route 46. So I followed them and they turned off on a dirt road into the back country. There in the middle of a beautiful pasture a barn was on fire. The deputies told me that the armored truck was in the barn and had burned too. What a mess that was. I guess everything was destroyed—the barn, the armored truck, not much left for the police to survey."

"One of the girls in the bank at Crystal Spring is a friend of mine and she told me she was really scared when those crooks began to shoot at the surveillance camera. She thought that they shot the old man at first, but then she realized that he was only hit with a fist because he jumped up so quickly and followed them out the rear door. Nobody has seen him since."

"I'll bet she was scared. I was—would have been too." Charlie gulped as he realized that he had almost given himself away. He felt his face flush as he stammered to talk his way out of trouble. "Did she see the faces of those big crooks? What did she say about that 'old geezer'?"

"No, she didn't see their faces and except for their size she couldn't identify any of them. She thought they were all young, big, strong, and seemed to have everything down to a science, with perfect timing. At least it was perfect till that old man got in the way. You do know that he had a wig on. My friend said that he almost lost it. He struggled to straighten it as he ran out the back."

"Did she tell the police that?"

"I don't know, but she said she thought his mustache looked fake too."

Gradually, the conversation turned away from the theft back to Joanne's daughter. She'd lost her husband recently and Joanne was trying to help her financially. It was obvious to Charlie that Joanne was not comfortable talking about all the troubles of her family.

"So, Charlie, where are you staying?"

"I'm in a time-share over near the golf course at Mineral City. My time is up next Saturday. Then I might spend a day or two here in town. In fact, I might stay a little longer if I can locate a good spot to stay," remarked Charlie. "My permanent home is in Florida, but I'm not really eager to go home. I recently lost my wife, so I really don't have a good reason to return home. Things sure do change in a hurry when you're old and you lose the one person in life that you depended on. The children try to fill the gap in my life but as you know, they can't take the place of your wife, lover, companion, and friend. I can't talk to them the way I talked to my wife. There are a lot of things I feel I should never tell them. Frankly, there are a lot of things in this world that should never be told, anyway."

"I think you're right, especially if others could be hurt by telling, Mr. Carson."

"Please call me Charlie. By the way, Joanne, please don't think I'm too forward, but you realize I'm getting old and as a result, I can't sit around waitin' until we get better acquainted to ask you to join me for dinner some night. I don't mean a fancy dinner, just out to Richard's or one of the other restaurants in High Prairie."

"Oh, that's very nice, Charlie, I'd be delighted. It has been very lonely for me since my husband died, and at my age I don't get many invitations. In fact, none at all if you want to know the truth."

"Well, I don't know why that should be. You're a lot younger than I am and besides you're much prettier," said Charlie. "Anyway, it's a date. Tomorrow night I'll pick you up about this time, when you get home from work. In the meantime, perhaps you could suggest a room that I might rent for a few days."

"That'd be fine and I'll certainly look for a room."

As he drove toward his condo, he was thinking that Joanne's house would make a perfect hideaway. No one would have any suspicion that he was staying there in the backwoods. Now, all he had to do was to talk her into an invitation. But how? Then, too, Joanne was really a delightful person and he had no desire to involve her in this escapade.

The next day, Charlie dressed in clean clothes with no wig or any other disguise. He drove into town to have breakfast at Johnny's Restaurant. The locals were deep in conversations with their friends while eating a hot steaming breakfast. Charlie made his way into a corner of the restaurant, waving to a few of the people that he recognized. His thoughts were centered around the fact that this town had certainly come alive. It used to be a sleepy country town, but now everyone seemed to be operating on full adrenaline. There were lines of people waiting to get a table. Many were imported police as well as local deputies. Then, too, there seemed to be an overload of tourists. Business was booming.

When Charlie finished eating, he walked across the street to Bobby Dee's porch. "Hey, Bobby," he called.

"Hi, Charlie. Join me. Come up and sit a spell. The town's so full of outsiders. By the way, Sheriff Macklin told me to tell you he'd like to talk to you."

"Talk to me? What for?"

"I don't know. But he said he saw your car the other day and he thought it sort of matched the one the "old geezer" was driving."

"Oh, hell. That's crazy."

"Charlie, quick, look over there. That big kid's lookin' at your car."

"Yeah, I see him. What the hell would he want with my car?" asked Charlie. "Tell me Bobby, have you heard anything about who set the fire out there at the Owens Barn?"

"No, nothing new," said Bobby Dee. "I haven't heard much except that the cops think the robbers never got the money. Somehow, the sheriff thinks, the robbers got ripped off. He believes that the robbers hid the armored track in the barn overnight, and then came back the next day to take the money. But when they returned, the money was gone, so they were so pissed off that they set fire to the whole damn works."

"But then, who got the money?" asked Charlie.

"Not sure, maybe that "old geezer" had something to do with it. Look, there's old Franklin across the street now. Do you know him?"

"Yeah, I gave him a lift the other day. Maybe he's the old man who was in the bank."

"No, Charlie, I've known him for years. He's a harmless old coot, who wouldn't hurt anyone. He is definitely short of genes in the head. Oh, by the way, I'd advise you to stop in to see the sheriff some time soon, 'cause he's like a bad winter's cold, you can never get rid of him. And he told me that he wanted to talk to you. Did you ever hear how he got to be sheriff?"

"No, but I guess I'll go see him next week."

Bobby Dee hardly allowed Charlie to answer. "I'd advise you not to try to put the sheriff off. Believe me, you don't want to anger him. Let me tell you the story of Sheriff Macklin's rise to power. When Tom Macklin was a youth, he lived with his mother and sister on a farm just north of High Prairie. His mother worked in a grocery store during the week and sold eggs to the various stores in town on weekends. Tom's father had walked out on the family years earlier, so the family had a hard time making ends meet. Well, sir," continued Bobby Dee, "Ella, Tom's mother, would pickup her paycheck on Saturday and with the cash from selling her eggs she would hide it in a draw of her desk. One Saturday, there was a knock at her screen door in the back of the house. Tom was thirteen years old and he was upstairs with country music playing on his radio. He paid no attention to the person who had come to the door. In the meantime, Tom's sister was playing in the front yard with a girlfriend of hers. For reasons that we don't know, Ella allowed the stranger to enter the house. Almost immediately, the stranger, who was a very large young man, attacked Ella. He made sexual advances, which were rejected. But when Ella attempted to scream, the stranger hit her with his massive fist, knocking her unconscious. Then he viciously raped her, causing her to bleed from both the sexual organs as well as from the blow to her head. The stranger searched the room and then the desk until he found all of the money that Ella had hidden in the draw. As the stranger casually walked out the back door while counting the money, Tom happened to see him from his bedroom window. Being inquisitive, Tom ran downstairs to see who had come to the house. The first thing he saw was that the desk had been rifled. Then he turn to see his mother, who was splattered with blood, laying on the couch. Tom screamed for his sister, 'Nelda, come quick! Help mom! I got to get that bastard.' Quick as a flash, he ran to the closet to get his father's pistol. He loaded it as he ran out the back door in search of the huge stranger. He saw the robber turn the corner of the barn. Tom ran, hell bent to capture that son-of-a-bitch, but as he rounded the corner, the robber smashed Tom with an old ax handle. The blow knocked Tom to the ground and for an instant or two he must have lost consciousness. When he awoke, all Tom saw was the huge stranger entering the field of corn. The corn was so tall that he could not see the man, but he could see the tops of the corn waving with every step that the stranger made. Tom made a quick decision to cut off the man's escape, so he ran to the edge of the corn field in the direction where he thought the man would exit the corn field. But the man cautiously peeked out from the stalks and saw Tom running toward him. The man then reversed direction, heading back to the barn. This time, when he came out, Tom threatened him with his pistol and warned him to halt. The man stopped, but backed his way toward the side of the barn to pickup the ax handle. Tom, although he was only thirteen, anticipated every move that the robber made. He knew that this big man would be extremely dangerous if he got close. So when the man made a lunge at Tom, Tom pulled the trigger. The bullet staggered the robber, but by instinct, the robber struck again. Tom fired his second shot, hitting the man again.

At this moment, Ella arrived at Tom's side to grab the pistol. She was yelling almost hysterically, 'Don't kill him! Don't kill him!' Ella tried to restrain Tom, but Tom was determined. He wiggled from Ella's grasp to run after the robber who had reached the tall corn stalks once again.

"Tom bolted after his prey with nothing but his bare hands. Ella and Tom's sister yelled frantically for Tom to give up the chase to no avail. Within a very few moments, Tom came out of the corn field pulling the stranger with one hand and waving the money that the man had stolen in his other. The end of the story is that this robber-rapist was sentenced to thirty years in jail and the sheriff invited Tom to help work around the police station. When he was old enough, he became a deputy and now, he has graduated to sheriff."

Charlie listened with admiration. He had gained a respect for this country boy. He knew now that it was necessary to take him seriously.

Bobby Dee continued to talk about all of the investigating agents that were arriving in town everyday. "The mayor of our little town told me yesterday that this thing has brought more business to town than it has ever had in the past. This is making our town known all over the world. If they can catch those robbers, the town will have something to talk about for years. It'll be a draw for tourists. I suppose it's like the old proverb— out of tragedy comes some good and every cloud has a silver lining, or something like that. Our town is certainly benefiting from all this publicity."

"Sheriff Macklin told me he believes he can wrap this mess up pretty quick. He seems to know more than we do, or else he's putting on a good act—I don't know which."

Charlie soon announced that he needed to head for home. He said, "That sheriff certainly sounds intelligent, as well as tenacious. He probably knows more than we could guess." Charlie shuddered as he walked away from Bobby Dee's real estate office.

A deep depression was overtaking Charlie. He felt the sheriff was beginning to close in on him and he had absolutely no idea what to do about it. Everything seemed to get more complicated all the time. These were the times that Charlie wished he had someone to confide in, someone such as his late wife. Charlie wondered whether he had asked too many questions or whether he had shown too much concern for the information that Bobby Dee was gathering from Sheriff Macklin.

When Charlie passed through the crossroads, he noticed the same red pick-up truck that had followed him the previous day pull on to Route 46 and immediately start to tailgate him. This time Charlie quickly increased the speed of his car.

"All right, you bastard, see if you can stay with me this time," Charlie bellowed out loud as his car responded to his foot pressing down harder and harder on the accelerator. Charlie seemed as if he were flying toward Mineral City, when he suddenly took a quick right toward Whisper Lake. He swung though the woods toward the end of the lake, but the truck still followed.

Charlie realized that the man in the red truck was a far better driver than Charlie had ever been. At least, he had much less fear of driving fast on these narrow, twisting mountain roads. The truck seemed to be gaining precious yards every time Charlie looked in his rearview mirror. Charlie felt as if he was screeching around every bend on two wheels and felt a sickening feeling in the pit of his stomach for he knew he could not increase his speed on these roads without experiencing panic.

As the two vehicles flashed through the back woods, Charlie's chances of outrunning his pursuer became ever smaller. "Son of a bitch," Charlie swore out loud, "I haven't got a chance against this bastard. I better duck down one of these dirt side roads—maybe I can lose him in the woods." Charlie swung his car around a sharp turn onto a dirt road that was little more than a path. The red truck slid to a halt just past the turn, forcing him to back up in order to make the turn. This gave Charlie a little extra distance ahead of the truck and a few extra moments to jump out of his car and scramble though the woods, up a steep hill, and down the other side to a pretty little stream that circled its way out of sight. Charlie was sweating like a bull and he was breathing like a marathon runner who had just crossed the finish line after a twenty-six-mile marathon. He slipped and slid his way along the stream until he was forced to stop to regain his breath. He crawled up under a thick laurel bush and plopped his backside in the cool wet mud. He could hear the young man following the path of the stream, heading in his direction. Cautiously, the young man approached Charlie's hide-out, while checking every bush that was large enough to hide a person.

It was obvious that the man would sooner or later find Charlie, and Charlie knew he was no match for this huge young man. He had to make a break for it and run deeper into the woods. His only chance was to get lost amongst the briars and tangled branches of the mountain laurel. He could wait no longer as he could now see the young man dogging his every step. On his hands and knees, Charlie crawled up a rather steep bank, scratching his face and catching his clothing from time to time. But gradually, he put a little distance between him and his skulking pursuer, who was meticulously following the path of the stream. The older man worked his way along a ridge toward a grove of trees, consisting of old gnarled trees supported by an extremely heavy undergrowth of tangled mountain laurel. He could hear the truck driver breaking though the brittle dry branches, coming in Charlie's direction. By this time, Charlie's shirt was torn and his clothing was covered with mud. As Charlie came to the trees, he realized his only chance was to climb up into the nearest tree in hopes that the truck driver would be scouring the undergrowth and never look up. With a great deal of effort, Charlie pulled himself up near the top branches of a tree and lay flat against the trunk. Within moments, he heard the man almost below him. Breathlessly, Charlie clung to the trunk and said a little prayer. "Lord, even though I don't deserve it, I need your help. I know I'm no match for this guy and this would be a lousy way to exit this world. Help me, Lord, and I'll make up for it."

The young brute poked a large stick into every deciduous, mossy bush that covered the area around this grove of trees. He worked his way back and forth as if he was sure that Charlie was hiding in the vicinity. Charlie was motionless and almost stopped breathing as the relentless youth worked his way directly under the tree. He stood motionless for several minutes, trying to listen for any noise from Charlie. But gradually, after no success, the young man wandered away and soon went out of sight and out of ear-shot.

Charlie waited for what seemed an eternity, hoping that the young man would become weary and give up the chase. Cautiously, Charlie climbed down from the tree, making his way back toward the car. He hesitated for an extended period, watching his own car to make sure that the young fellow had driven off in the red truck. At last, it appeared safe for Charlie to get into his car and speed for home. He had a little trouble turning the car around on this narrow path, but then he swung on to the main road. He felt confident that he could make it home safely.

Without warning, the red truck appeared in his rearview mirror. At this point, Charlie realized that out there in the bushes and the backwoods the advantage had once again swung over to the red truck. Even though he had separated from the truck by a few hundred feet, he couldn't shake him. He decided that he would be safer around some other people, so he headed toward the golf course. When he saw the beautiful fairway ahead of him, he threw caution to the wind and drove his car into the middle of the third fairway. The truck was hanging hard on his tail. Charlie's car tore up some of the grass but there was no turning back now, so he swung up the hill onto the next fairway. The truck seemed to be gaining on him. Abruptly, Charlie swung down toward the waterfall near the small meadow. He knew that if he could cross this meadow in the one narrow path that was usually dry, then perhaps he could lose that damned truck. He had played golf here many times and he knew where the dry spot was. The truck driver probably wouldn't know, so he might get stuck in the soggy meadow.

Charlie drove across the dry path, then mounted the hill next to the waterfall and suddenly he was back on the blacktop road. The truck was attempting to cut off Charlie's route when at the last moment, the driver realized that he was headed into the soggy grass. He skidded on the wet grass and came to rest in ankle-deep water. He spun his wheels long enough for Charlie to drive out of sight.

At last, Charlie was free. He circled up the mountain with a sigh of relief because he was able to get back to his time-share without any fear of facing whoever was in that damn red truck.

Glad to be back in his condo, Charlie turned on the TV and sunk into a chair to see the afternoon news. A local reporter announced, "And now, we'll hear from our star reporter in Falon, North Carolina."

"Good afternoon, ladies and gentlemen. Today, the Falon Police announced the capture of a young man who caused a ruckus in a bar last night. The young man said he had been ripped off by an old man with a beard and mustache. The young man, who was drunk, claimed he had millions of dollars that were taken from him by the old man." The news reporter continued with the story. "The police immediately contacted the sheriff in charge of the theft in Crystal Springs, who appeared interested in questioning the young man. The sheriff indicated that perhaps his theory, that the old man in the bank had stolen the money from the robbers, might be true."

The more that Charlie listened to the news, the more he became concerned about his predicament. It had become imperative in Charlie's mind to either buy a new car or at least, have his car washed and polished. Too many people were connecting his car with the dirty car that the "old geezer" was driving. When Charlie and Joanne returned to her house after having a delightful dinner together, she immediately extended an offer to Charlie that he couldn't refuse. "Charlie, you said that your time is up at the time share, why don't you use my extra room? Move in as soon as you wish."

"That's great. I've been wondering where I could go. I really appreciate that."

"With that settled, let's take a walk."

"Okay, where to?"

"Just along the old logging road."

As they walked the lonely road, darkness crept in like a thief in the night. But Charlie knew exactly where they were, in the area of the waterfalls.

"Look at that light, right there, see it? There, through the trees."

"Yeah, Charlie, I thought I heard some voices too."

"Who the hell would be out here in the dark?"

"I'll bet someone is working the still tonight. I've heard rumors about it."

"Oh, let's sneak closer and see what's going on."

"Okay. Come on, let's go."

Quietly, the two worked their way through the woods until they could clearly see and hear two men sitting near the kerosene lantern. Joanne spoke first in a whisper, "That's Franklin, you know, Franklin Delano Roose."

"Who's the guy he's talking too?"

"Everybody knows Franklin, but I'm not sure who the other one is."

"Listen," said Charlie, "Can you hear what they are talking about?"

"Jeremiah," said Franklin, "Fill 'er up again, *mmm*. That sho is good. That's the best you ever made. You's gitten better all the time."

"Smooth ain't it?"

"Smoother than a baby's butt. That's just as smooth as that 'old geezer' who suckered them, young robbers."

"I thought that was you in the bank at first."

"Nah."

"Who else could-a-done it?"

"Maybe that old guy, you know, the friend of Bobby Dee. He's about the right size and he pushes his hair back in place the way the 'old geezer' did on the tape at the bank when it was being robbed."

"How'd you know that, Frank?"

"Not sure," said Franklin as he pulled on his beard while making believe that he was in deep thought. "I met him on the road one day. He gave me a lift to the crossroads, and he looked like he fit the bill."

"Is that the old bastard whose callin' on Mrs. Botts, down the road?"

"Yeah, that's him."

"Well, he knows the area, and maybe he's plannin' to grab the loot and Mrs. Botts and runnin' outta here together."

When Charlie heard this scenario, he looked at Joanne and whispered, "I never thought of that, did you?"

"No, but then I didn't know that you were involved in that bank robbery."

"I'm not. But I admit I like the idea."

"Charlie, you sly dog, is that an invitation?"

"What if it was?"

"Well, I'd have to think about it. I'm the kind who can't make a big decision like that in a hurry. You and the money—boy, that's a combination."

"I can't make a fast decision either, but this sure has great possibilities, with or without the money."

"Charlie, Charlie, are you telling me that you stole the money?"

"Hell no! Do I look like that 'old geezer'?"

"No, not to me, but sometimes I have the feeling that you're covering up something that you would like to get off your chest."

"Well, I do have something on my mind and one day I will probably tell you all about it."

Their conversation had gradually gotten louder than a whisper when Charlie noticed that the two men were looking in his direction.

"Quiet, they'll hear us." Charlie and Joanne nestled quickly into the leaves in order to duck out of sight.

Jeremiah stood up and peered into the darkness but finally, he was satisfied that no one was in the vicinity, so he poured another drink for himself and his partner.

Joanne and Charlie listened for a few minutes more but the men's conversation became less than interesting, until Joanne suggested that she and Charlie retreat to her home.

All at once, Charlie burst out laughing. He often could see the funny side of life. "Can you imagine, two old farts crawling around in a thick woods at night, spying on two moonshiners. That's some picture!"

"Certainly we're old enough to know better, but anyway, I'll expect you to move into my extra room any time you want."

# Nine

The rain only lasted a short while, during the night, but it was enough to make the roads slippery. The fresh green leaves danced with dew in the morning light, as Charlie drove into Crystal Springs to retrieve some mail from the general delivery window at the post office. The town was overly busy with the tourists and the extra law enforcement officers that had been assigned to this case. Charlie wormed his way though the traffic only to find that most of the parking spaces were taken, especially around the post office. Standing in line at the stamp window was as uncommon as the line of people that were waiting to get into Johnny's Restaurant for breakfast.

As Charlie made his way back into town, he saw Bobby Dee already sitting in his rocking chair. He was in his customary position, overseeing everything that happened in town.

"Hey, Charlie. How ya doin?" asked Bobby.

"Good, Bobby," answered Charlie.

"Come on up and sit a spell."

Charlie nodded, then climbed the steps to plunk himself in the extra rocker.

"Is this reserved for me?" he questioned.

"You might as well use it. Wait a minute, I think my phone is ringing. I better get it, maybe it could be a client," said Bobby Dee as he walked into his office.

Bobby answered with a loud "Hello, Yeah, Good morning sheriff. Yup! Yes! Where? You mean near Big Falls? Oh, my God! Sure I'll go. Yeah, I have a winch on the front of my truck with about two hundred feet of cable. Sure. Right now, just as quick as I can. You bet," answered Bobby as he hung up the phone.

"Come on, Charlie, maybe you can help. You know that I'm a volunteer on the rescue squad. Well, Sheriff Macklin just called to tell me that a boy has fallen over one of the cliffs near Big Falls.

They need my truck in a hurry to help pull him out. Come on, let's go."

Charlie sprung from his rocker as if obeying a military command. He ran quickly to Bobby Dee's huge new pick-up truck. The front seat seemed extra wide inside, in fact, it was plenty wide enough for three large men. The entire truck seemed oversized to Charlie. There were double tires in the rear and the hood was long enough to house a sixteen-cylinder motor. The dashboard had a lot of additional equipment including a two-way radio. Behind Charlie's head a thirty-gauge rifle hung in a rack. It was an intimidating looking gun and it hung in a most convenient place.

Almost before Charlie had settled in his seat, Bobby Dee switched on a screeching siren and put a flashing red light on the roof. He weaved though traffic with the skill of a New York taxi driver. Moments later the truck was traveling down the wet road past High Knob at a speed that Charlie would never attempt. Bobby was driving like a professional race car driver. At times, Charlie had to steady himself by grabbing on to the armrest. He was lucky to be strapped in, and with every mile Bobby Dee's demeanor became more serious. He was dedicated to his mission, and now, Charlie could see that Bobby Dee demanded obedience.

Suddenly, Bobby swung his big truck off the main road onto a gravel road that headed up one steep incline after another. "Sheriff Macklin told me on the phone that a couple of kids were trying to fly a kite from one of the cliffs that overlooks Big Falls," Bobby said. "There was a man fishing for trout at the bottom of the gorge. He saw two kids out on the edge of the cliff trying to fly their kite. As he watched, one of the boys suddenly slipped, falling to the brush below. From there, he bounced off the thick underbrush onto the domed-rock below. Of course, when he hit that, he slid off the edge and landed on a small shelf below the rock face. I don't think we can get to that area from below. We'll lower someone down to the rock face in order to traverse down to the ledge where the boy is. Fortunately, the fisherman had a portable phone with him. He has been in a position to guide us to the boy. He said that the boy hadn't moved since he fell."

It only took a few more minutes for Bobby to maneuver his truck up a steep embankment to a flat area on the edge of the cliff. Most of the volunteer men of the rescue squad were already there, and were in the process of preparing a plan to lower a man down to the thicket. Then it would be necessary for someone to cut a path, or at least an opening, down to the rock.

"Bob," called the deputy in charge of the operation, "Pull your truck front-first right up to the edge so we can use your winch to lower someone down." Turning toward the rest of the men he called, "We need someone to cut a path. Who have we got here?"

"Where's Red? Red Kaufinan, where are you?" someone shouted, "He's the only one that can handle this."

Red stepped forward.

Charlie was aghast. Red was a giant. He had huge shoulders and arms as big as most men's legs, but his most distinguishing feature was his wavy red hair. He was at least six-feet-six and seemed to be made of steel. Charlie imagined that when this man swung a machete, a small tree winced. With unbelievable speed, several members of the squad helped Red into a harness and hooked him to the cable on the front of Bobby's truck. They easily lowered Red down to the thick brush where Red cut a swath through the woods. At times, I could hear Red's booming voice calling up to his cohorts, "Lower me a little more."

Charlie had positioned himself near one of the team, "Couldn't you call for a helicopter? It might be an easier way to get to the boy."

"Listen, old man, you go over there and stay there, then you won't be in our way," was the only answer that Charlie got.

It was like a sharp knife to the heart, for it was suddenly apparent that because of his age, Charlie's services were no longer needed. He was made to realize in one short moment that the world was leaving him behind. Youth, strength, and clear thinking had usurped the position that he had held for many years. This proved to be just one more time that Charlie was forced to relinquish the reins. During the last few months, he had yielded one thing after another to the changing times.

Now, Charlie stood watching the big redhead chop his way through the brush. It was easy to tell that time was pressing on the entire squad because every one of them was working at a rapid pace. Red frantically worked his way down to the domed rock, but when he attempted to stand, the rock proved to be too steep. It was lucky that he was tethered to the truck or he would have gone over the cliff with the boy.

Bobby Dee carefully let out the cable, inch by inch. The radio in the truck was blaring loud reports from Sheriff Macklin, who was relaying reports from the fisherman in the gorge below. "Work to your right. You'll miss the boy if you go straight down," repeated Sheriff Macklin. "You have at least fifty more feet to go. Have you got enough cable?"

Bobby answered loud enough for the sheriff to hear without the phone, "Yep. We've got at least seventy feet left."

Everyone was working efficiently, and Charlie could see that this team had practiced endless hours in order to become so proficient, even though they were only volunteers.

Moments later, Red called out, "He's alive! Send the basket down!" At the top, Al Hemple was preparing to descend through the small opening that Red had chopped with his ax and machete. Al had been picked for this job primarily because of his diminutive size. He worked his way through the trees and the underbrush until he reached the rock face, where he established a firm foothold in order to lower the basket down to Red who had crawled out on the ledge.

Red strapped the boy into the basket and then gave a loud yell for Bobby to haul away. Slowly the basket, which at times was almost vertical, inched its way up the rock with Red guiding it. Moments had become minutes, and now minutes had become almost an hour. Charlie, after watching the rescue for such a long time, turned toward the magnificent view of the waterfall and he walked over to the other boy who had also been flying the kite. Charlie made a gesture of friendliness to the boy by putting his arm around the boy's shoulder. This opened the door to the emotions that the boy had been withholding ever since his friend fell. When Charlie asked the boy what his name was, the boy sobbed out a name that was barely audible. "Chuck."

"No kidding," said Charlie. "That's my name too, only they call me Charlie." Immediately, there was a bond forming between the old and the young.

Charlie tried to reassure Chuck that his friend was going to make it. "Come on, Chuck, stick with me. These guys in the rescue squad don't need us. They'll save your friend without our help but we need each other, they don't need us. They would probably rather not have us here anyway." There wasn't much for Charlie to say to encourage the young man but Charlie kept talking in order to occupy the boy's mind. "Come on, let's walk over there nearer the edge where they'll bring him up. He'll make it, you'll see."

At last, the boy began to say a few things, "I didn't see him fall, Jimmy yelled and I looked around and he was gone. I didn't know what happened."

With both Al and Red steadying the basket, it was a slow process returning the boy to the top of the cliff.

When the basket nosed over the crest, all the other members of the team who were not active at this moment sprang into service. Within seconds, they had the boy attached to an IV and splints put on various parts of his body. When they slid the boy into the back of the ambulance, the medic commented for everyone's benefit, "He's coming to now! I'm sure he'll make it okay."

The radio in Bobby Dee's truck was still blurting out more orders, "Bobby Dee, where the hell are you? Come in, Bobby!" The sheriff was as persistent as a child asking for candy.

Bobby calmly walked over to the radio picked up the mike and answered in his rather droll manner, "Yeah, what's up, Sheriff?"

"Listen, Bobby," demanded the sheriff, "There's been another accident on the road to Sparta. You're the only one close to it. Grab Deputy Sam and his car and get there as quick as you can. I'm told that there are some injuries. I'll meet you there as quick as I can with another ambulance. I think you're about three miles away. Hurry up! I'll see you there."

The sheriff didn't even wait for an answer from Bobby as he cut off the radio.

Once again, Bobby jumped into action. "Hey, Sam, you heard him. Let's go. You too, Charlie! We've got another emergency!"

The deputy bolted to his car to follow Bobby and Charlie in the truck. They peeled out and nearly flew over the dirt roads toward the main route. Charlie bounced from side to side while he tried to hook up his seat belt. Both drivers turned away from Crystal Springs toward Sparta. Charlie thought Bobby had driven fast before, but this time his speed was ludicrous.

As they approached a dangerous curve, Charlie noticed skid marks on the blacktop road, and just below the embankment, he could see the tail end of a car sticking up. The deputy hit his brakes, coming to a screeching halt. Both the deputy and Bobby were out of their vehicles in a flash, followed by a slower-moving Charlie.

The car had obviously run through the curve, and then jumped over the embankment to hit a tree. Three people were inside, and Charlie could see blood all over the inside of the car. Both the Deputy and Bobby struggled to pry the door open. Immediately, Bobby attempted to take the pulse of a young girl who was obviously severely hurt. Bobby pressed his fingers on her neck. Then he placed them on her temple. There was no pulse in either place, so Bobby reached for her wrist. After a slight hesitation, he said, "Oh, shit! I don't feel any pulse at all. She must be dead! Sam, let's work on the other two. I can see that they're both alive. Charlie, you take the dead girl out of the car, so she's out of our way." Charlie obeyed at once, but in order to move her bloody body he had to pull her against his chest with a maximum effort and then drag her limp body under a nearby tree. When he laid her body down with a great deal of care, he judged that she was about sixteen years old. He wiped the blood off her face with his handkerchief.

She looked so peaceful lying there that Charlie felt compassion that almost overwhelmed him. Spontaneously, he reacted to the situation and began mouth to mouth resuscitation. He tried and tried. It seemed hopeless and final, when he heard a siren, apparently from the sheriff's car, in the distance. He knew he couldn't stop now. If there was any chance, he must keep going until the ambulance arrived. Charlie didn't want to give up anyway, but he was losing faith, for there had been no response from the limp figure lying on the cold ground.

Suddenly, he thought he heard a small sigh from the young girl. His heart raced and his spirit rose. Maybe there was still a chance.

In the meantime, Bobby and the deputy had extricated the two surviving young people and were extending first aid to both. The ambulance arrived at the scene, allowing both the sheriff and the medic to leap to the aid of Bobby and the deputy.

Charlie yelled in-between breaths, "Medic, help me! I think she's breathing, I can't keep going much longer."

Both the medic and the sheriff ran to Charlie's aid. The sheriff was an impressive man. He was big and strong with broad shoulders and a classic Roman profile. His hands were as big as a catcher's mitt. His long strides carried him quickly to Charlie's side. With one graceful but powerful move he picked up Charlie like a rag doll so that he could see the young girl more clearly. "My God," he cried, "My God, it's my daughter! She's breathing! Medic, get the oxygen."

Charlie smiled as he withdrew from the girl. One thought entered his mind. Maybe his life wasn't superfluous. His useless, outdated, old-age life had some value to it after all. He then walked toward Bobby to see if there was anything else he might do.

During his younger life, he felt much more important because he had built a fine small lumber yard and molding mill in which he employed 50 people. Consequently, the decisions he made were all his and they were made with logic and practicability. Naturally, he had Ethyl, his wife, who backed him implicitly.

But now, old age was robbing him of his self reliance and the death of his wife had stolen his foundation and support. Every decision at this age looked momentous and unsolvable. In addition, annoyances were creeping into his life. Now, when he threw his clothing in a heap on his chair, no one was around to hang them up. He found that it was a great effort to keep a neat tidy house. And he discovered that this was true for many other things in his life.

Even his idiosyncrasies were now exposed, for there was no longer any one who loved him enough to help cover them up, such as his habit of pulling on the lobe of his ear when he had a decision to make.

"Life at this stage of life is most certainly downhill," Charlie murmured. "The yearning for youth goes well beyond the physical aspect, more to the mental."

# Ten

Charlie relaxed on the porch of his condominium, which overlooked the beautiful fairway of the golf course. He felt very comfortable with a scotch and water in his hand while the evening twilight crept down from the mountain tops. This was the sort of setting that he enjoyed the most. Unfortunately, they were few and far between. He reminisced about the many times he had played this beautiful golf course. Like many golfers, Charlie's memory of his talents was greater than the actual skill that he had exhibited on the golf course. But that seemed all right to Charlie, for certain memories become embellished over the years.

Just about the time that his thoughts turned to his past life, Charlie was jarred out of his musings by a voice from the next apartment. "Charlie," called Jeff, "How about trying our luck fishing tomorrow? We could start downstream below the falls and work our way back toward them. Now, don't say no! You have nothing to do tomorrow and we need a little excitement."

At first, Charlie stammered, but finally settled himself because he knew that he couldn't say no. He had no genuine excuse. "Okay, Jeff. That sounds like fun! Do you want to go in the morning?"

"No, afternoon would be better for me."

"Fine, I'll pick you up at one o'clock."

The balance of the evening was left to Charlie's favorite memories of his life with his wife and children. His thoughts were uninterrupted since there was nothing new on the TV concerning the robbery.

By 1 P.M. the next day, Charlie was knocking on Jeff's door. "Come on, Jeff. There's a monstrous trout that has been waiting all morning for you to drop your line in the water. Let's go."

"Yeah, and I'll bet you told that monster not to touch my line," replied Jeff, as he slid his lanky frame into the front seat of

Charlie's car. "Today, we're going to keep moving upstream toward the waterfall until we catch something worthwhile."

As Charlie drove his car up the old logging trail, he realized how close they were to Joanne's home. So he made an effort to lead Jeff in the opposite direction until at last they reached the fast-flowing stream.

It wasn't long before Jeff was casting into various little pools of water in search of the monster. As Jeff's patience grew short, he kept insisting that the two men work their way up stream nearer the falls. Gradually, Charlie grew more and more stubborn against approaching the waterfalls. His worry increased with every step closer to the mud bank where Charlie had buried his treasure.

"Charlie, I've got a hunch that the monster is sleeping under a rock in the big pool just beneath the waterfalls. Come on, let's go find out."

Charlie delayed as much as he could without creating suspicion that he was hiding something from Jeff. Soon the two men had caught their share of trout and arrived within sight of the falls. Charlie immediately announced that he felt it was time to retreat back downstream.

"Charlie, what's with you today?" asked Jeff, but there was no answer. Jeff continued to prod Charlie again and again. "Every time I suggest going to the pool under the falls, you object. *Me thinks you doth protest too much*—or whatever that old saying used to be."

Charlie, who was reeling in his fishing line, froze in a bent position. Panic swept over him, for he felt that Jeff had suddenly peeled off his mask and his naked thoughts were exposed. Fortunately, Jeff was far enough away that he couldn't see Charlie's face flush, but Jeff recognized Charlie's physical reaction to his question. Jeff stood for a moment contemplating what he had observed, "Listen Charlie, if I've pushed too much, I apologize. It just seemed to me that you're a little uptight today."

Charlie turned away in order to keep Jeff from scrutinizing his face. It wasn't often that Charlie was caught off guard. To be questioned by his good friend had thrown Charlie off balance. The expression on Jeff's face was enough for Charlie to withdraw his request. Charlie chuckled in order to soften the tension and replied, "Now you're off your rocker, Jeff."

At this moment, both men could hear noises coming from an area near the waterfalls. Charlie strained to distinguish the sounds. At first, it sounded like a lot of birds, but gradually Charlie realized that it was the voices of several children playing in and out of the waterfalls. At the same time Jeff came to the same conclusion and said, "Let's go see what they're up to."

Fear now gripped Charlie, once again. Now, he realized how vulnerable his hiding spot was. It was obvious that he must find a new spot to bury his windfall.

Jeff continued to speak, "These kids come up here all the time to swim in this little pond and play under the falls. These are the times, I wish I was young again. I'd love to go join them."

Charlie joined in Jeff's wishes. "Those were great days, when we didn't have a care in the world. I guess we can't go back, but maybe we can make it better for our offspring." The two men reminisced for several minutes, when at last Charlie announced that he was beginning to get a little weary. "You know, Jeff, ever since Ethyl died, I seem to run out of juice more often and earlier than I used to. Who knows, maybe it just is old age, but whatever it is, I don't like it. If you don't mind, I think we'd better start heading for home. We'll catch that monster next time." Then Charlie developed another image in his mind. He envisioned one of the kids playing near the falls stumbling over the money bags and Charlie's whole secret becoming exposed.

When the men arrived home, Charlie switched on the TV and changed channels until he found one that was giving the local evening news. Sheriff Macklin was being interviewed. "Let me explain," the sheriff continued, "in order to make sure that we are doing everything in our power to solve this robbery and the location of the money, we have hired a psychic in hopes that she might be able to lead us to the millions of stolen money. After an hour of meditation, Madam Irena Chiran claimed she had a very strong psychic experience. Let me quote her so that I cannot be misunderstood. She said, 'The money is hidden in an area where children play.'"

The prophecy shocked Charlie so severely that he almost fell off the chair. He literally jumped from his chair and yelled out loud, "My God, how'd she know that?" It was now imperative that the money bags be moved, but where could he hide them?

All night, Charlie wrestled with this new problem. If he decided to split up the money, then he would need two hiding spots. That made it twice as hard. Every place that came to his mind was fraught with flaws. He even reviewed the original locations that he had considered when he first hid the money. The night slipped by until just before dawn, when he suddenly sat up in bed. "I know where I'll hide it. I'll go back to the burned out barn and scratch around there in the burned out portion, until I can find enough remnants to cover the bags or the ice chests." He jumped from his bed, slipped on some clothing, grabbed his shovel and his flashlight, and set out in his car for the Owens' barn. This ought to be a good spot to hide it, for the sheriff and most of the townfolks had already searched the area for money and clues. It didn't seem likely to Charlie that anyone would search there again. As he drove toward the barn, he planned to use his shovel to prepare a spot so that some night he would make a trip to the waterfalls, grab the money, and quickly travel to the old barn to deposit it in its new hiding place. The dawn was already breaking so that he was afraid to move it in the daylight. He was convinced that he must move the treasure under the cover of darkness, and that meant that he must choose a night when no one would know where he was or what he was doing.

His efforts at scraping away the burned charcoal left him exhausted, but at least he had prepared an excellent hiding spot. Charlie covered everything around the cold storage bin with partially burned beams and charcoal until it wasn't visible to anyone who might be passing by. Then he returned to his car and proceeded to drive to the main road. Around the first of many bends in the road stood his acquaintance, Franklin Delano Roose. He was in the same dirty clothes, and Charlie was sure that he hadn't washed since their last meeting. Charlie couldn't drive by without stopping to talk. Franklin was standing next to a tremendous tree that had a large hole on one side of its trunk. Charlie stopped his car to call out to Franklin, "Hey, Frank, what in hell are you doing out here this early in the morning?"

"Well sur, I'm picking up my mail in this old tree. This is my private mail box. Then I'm heading to my home up there on the mountain. I spent the night at the jail in High Prairie as a guest of my esteemed sheriff."

"Oh, what did you do wrong?" asked Charlie.

"Well sur. He thought that I was in the bank when it was robbed. But the sheriff knows that I never tell a lie and I never chopped down that cherry tree. That wasn't me in the bank, but I have my own idea about who it is, don't you, Mr. Carson? When we get old there is a bond between all old people. We can read the souls of our contemporaries because we use imagination, and imagination is the eyes of the soul but one must focus it . . ."

Charlie laughed out loud, for he suddenly felt exposed to a stranger. What does this mountain man know? He seems to piece unrelated things into a tightly knit scheme. Besides, this old coot was doing it again. He loves to make reference to quotations from our past presidents, but he twists them and alters them to suit himself. "Franklin," asked Charlie, trying to change the subject, "aren't you afraid to walk these back roads in the dark? Maybe an animal might attack you or you might get sick out here all alone."

"Well Sur, with malice toward none and with charity for all, I walk softly and carry a big stick," quoted the old mountain man, combining parts of Lincoln's speech with Teddy Roosevelt's.

"Mr. Carson, Sur!" Franklin continued, "In the house of the righteous is much treasure: but in the revenues of the wicked is trouble. That's Proverb 15-6."

"Goodbye, Frank." Then under his breath, Charlie expressed some self-disgust. "My God, we've been on this earth about the same number of years and I have a feeling of superiority. Am I a snob? A bigot? I was never brought up to be one. My father was a Quaker who taught us to accept everyone—young or old, smart or dumb, rich or poor, black or white. It doesn't matter! No, I don't think I'm a snob, maybe I just don't understand the human race. Age produces so many new doubts and questions that seemed so easy and clear when I was young. Enough of that, I'll worry about that tomorrow. My worry, today, concerns

Frank. Soon, I'll have to move my treasure to a new location, perhaps to the food cellar at Owens' old barn. Then Frank won't have any idea of where I've hidden my treasure. He certainly has intuitive powers."

# Eleven

The amount of activity in town the next morning was unprecedented. The Trolley Station Restaurant had resembled a miniature train station where the specialty of the house was soup and sandwiches, but now the new specialty was police, FBI agents, and cop cars. The sheriff and his law enforcement officers took over the station to use it as a mobile command post. The workers from the power company and the TV were in the same area. There were more trucks behind the bank than he'd ever seen. More police came in order to control the power company and TV workers as well as the sightseers. The back parking lot of the bank was the best spot for TV cameras because they could keep a constant surveillance of all activities around the bank. By panning the cameras to the north, the crossroads came into view.

Charlie came to town to find that he had to wind his way through miles of cable and electrical lines to visit his friend. Bobby was sitting on his porch in his usual chair, watching all the activities in town. Traffic was bumper to bumper from Bobby's office all the way to the crossroads. "Bobby," said Charlie, "You look like you're the master of all you survey. From your vantage point you could probably direct traffic."

"Yeah, it's beginning to look like the Superbowl crowd."

"I saw a young boy, selling shirts and balloons with 'Theft of the Century' written on them and a picture of gold coins spilling out of a money bag. I wish we could think something up and sell them right from your porch here. I'm sure the merchants here in town are thrilled with the amount of business they're doing. This town is going nuts," observed Charlie.

"This is the largest robbery ever in North Carolina, and perhaps the largest in the south. Last night, there was an emergency meeting of the town council and all the merchants in town to see whether they could prolong this thing so the tourists would keep coming back even after the sheriff solves the crime.

With enough publicity and hoopla, the mayor envisioned this could become an annual affair. People sure love excitement like this, especially if that 'old geezer' had something to do with it," commented Bobby Dee. "Yesterday evening, I heard that there are a lot of young people searching the backwoods near the area that they found the burned-out armored truck, hoping to find a clue to the hiding place of the money. Every one seems to think that if the "old geezer" took the money, he couldn't have hidden it very far away."

"You know, I'll bet if old man Owens was still alive, he'd be patrolling his farm with a double barrel shotgun. Did you know old man Owens, Bobby?" asked Charlie.

"Sure, I knew him. He was a tough old mountain man. He'd scare the hell out of anyone with one eye going off in one direction and the other boring right through you. His family was one of the original families that settled in this valley, that's how he got that beautiful piece of property. Oh, by the way, did you ever have that talk with the sheriff, Charlie? He said that the "old geezer" was definitely wearing a disguise and he thought that you might have seen him or know where he's holed up. For some reason, perhaps your dirty old car, the sheriff has a feeling that there is some connection between you and that "old geezer." Why don't you stop in and satisfy the sheriff?"

"No. I haven't seen him since we met at the accident on the road to Sparta and he was too busy to talk then. Besides, Bobby, I don't know a damn thing, anyway." Charlie continued to talk in hopes of getting Bobby's mind off that subject. "How is the sheriff's daughter doin'?"

"Very well, especially after being so close to death," answered Bobby Dee. "I was proud of all you guys at the Cliffs, and at the accident. You all acted like trained professionals."

Again, he wanted to change the direction of the conversation so he made a new comment, "Who'd believe this town could change so dramatically overnight? I'll bet that most of the locals love the excitement and I'll bet they secretly hope the crooks getaway with it."

"Nah, I think they'd like to see the old man get away with it but not the crooks. They have a funny moral attitude. They'll cheer for the underdog as long as they think they could benefit, somehow, but if they don't see a possible benefit then they'll become holier than thou and demand justice for the culprit. Right now, they feel that the only outcome for this town will be to draw a lot of extra tourists for years. To them that's the best possible result."

"I guess we all want a little extra for ourselves, and to increase the number of visitors to the town isn't too much to ask for," agreed Charlie.

"Bill over at Exxon has rented a bus. He's selling a local tour from Mineral City to Whitewater Falls and from High Prairie to Falon. O'course the tour will end here at the bank with all the details of the robbery. I suppose the tour will die as soon as they catch the guilty ones."

"I heard they caught one of them in Falon, yesterday," said Charlie.

"Yeah, Sheriff Macklin told me today that the young man is beginning to talk. I'm sure the cops will keep interrogating him until he tells all he knows. He has already admitted that he believes some old man stole all the money he had, which apparently was a great deal. Fred, the bank manager, told me the merchants suggested we build a statue in the middle of the crossroads, a statue of the "old geezer" holding up three robbers. It would be kinda funny, wouldn't it?"

"Boy, this is really getting out of hand. I never realized how greedy people could be," said Charlie.

"Yeah, even now there are a lot of young men searching the woods and mountains for that money and you know as well as I do, if they find it they'll never turn it in. In fact, I wish I had a chance at it," replied Bobby Dee.

"I guess we all have a little larceny in us," confirmed Charlie. "Mark Twain wrote 'Every man is a moon and has a dark side which he never shows to anyone'."

"I really don't know what I'd do if I found it. It'd be a damn hard decision. I might have to do a lot of thinking about what I could do to hide it."

"I know what I'd do," said Charlie.

"Unless I miss my guess, I think you might want to steal the money, but in the long run and at your age, I think you'd turn it back in," replied Bobby.

There was a long hesitation by both men. Both were considering what they would do but neither wanted to admit too much.

Bobby Dee finally said, "I guess the determining question has to be, 'can I get away with it?' Most people have a crooked streak in them, especially if there is a good chance of not getting caught. O'course one of the guiding factors is that if you getaway with it, you will be fabulously wealthy and that, in turn, would change your children's lives as well as your own. I suspect that even you might think about it more than twice."

Charlie wiggled in his chair. He wished to find out more of what Bobby knew, but now, Bobby's conversation was making him very uncomfortable. "It's time for me to get going," he said, "I've got a lot to do before supper time."

"Pioneer Day is Saturday. The main events are going to be held over there near the library. Are you going?" asked Bobby Dee.

"I guess so. I love to watch those young bucks chopping wood and pitching horseshoes. And I love the little kids in the egg throwing contest." Then Charlie turned with a half salute to step off the porch and was once again swallowed up by the mob of visitors who had come to see the crime scene.

Bobby Dee was right, Charlie's conscience was chewing on his mind. Charlie's main fear was the loss of his reputation for honesty and integrity. He went to a public phone near the supermarket to call Joanne and ask her to dinner.

"Sure," was her cheerful answer. "Pick me up at seven o'clock."

Seven o'clock came and Charlie was still trying to clear his mind of all the negative thoughts that had crept into his psyche. He had dressed in his dark sports coat and even put on a tie. When Joanne came to the door he was impressed that she was dressed so beautifully. He knew she was a fine-looking woman, but dressed in her red silk suit she was "class."

Joanne and Charlie drove along Route 17 which is a gorgeous road, until they arrived at the entrance to Knob Hill. There were big boxwood plants on either side of the driveway and blooming rhododendrons as a backdrop. In the distance, you could see parts of a groomed golf course. The driveway continued to wander up a hill to the front door of the clubhouse. Huge old trees with colossal trunks and branches that hung over the roof seemed to create a setting that could be used in the movie, *Gone with the Wind*. Charlie had read in the local paper that this magnificent house was the oldest in Crystal Springs and that it had been built by a southern general before the Civil War.

The clubhouse was built of wood, and some of the clapboards still had bark clinging on them and lots of moss on the roof. Inside, the wooden floors squeaked with each step, and at the end of the room stood a tremendous stone fireplace. In the dining room, there were no rugs on the floors and the chairs were straight and stiff. It was not conducive to casual, quiet dining, but the food was excellent.

Charlie and Joanne turned the keys of the car over to the valet, then took comfortable rocking chairs on the porch with a drink until their dinner was ready. Charlie reminisced about how he and his late wife enjoyed a dinner at a high-class dining room, even though they only went occasionally. Joanne and Charlie both agreed that they were each delighted to be partners in this dining out.

Their conversation was delightful, and it was about insignificant subjects with nothing said about the robbery. It was a time for the pair to get to know each other. The more they talked, the more each enjoyed the other. They talked about their respective families as well as their personal hopes and dreams. They had personalities that seemed to dovetail perfectly.

Dinner was so pleasant, and Charlie was delighted to see that Joanne was enjoying it too. With the end of dinner, Charlie suggested that they take a walk along the edge of the nearby lake.

It was a perfect setting for young lovers, with the cool evening breeze blowing off the lake and the fresh smell of newly mowed grass. But these two people were not young lovers, nor were they lovers at all. They both knew and understood this. Their respect for each other had not vaulted into love. However, they walked down the path closer and closer until at last, Joanne slipped her arm through Charlie's. Then she waited for a comment.

Charlie looked down at Joanne, hesitated for a moment, and then said, "That feels very natural and pleasant."

"Yes it does, doesn't it?" asked Joanne. "You know that Pioneer Day is this Saturday. Would you like to go? I think we would enjoy it together."

"Yeah, I'd love to," answered Charlie, "I'll watch the contests and you can judge the quilting. I'm not too much for going through every one of those booths to see someone's handiwork—like cutting a rabbit out of a piece of wood."

"You mean you don't like the talents of our local residents?" chided Joanne.

"I mean I don't like to waste my time looking at something like crocheting that I know nothing about and don't care to learn. I'd rather spend my time watching the kids running in the potato-sack race," answered Charlie.

"I guess I agree, but maybe we ought to get dressed up in pioneer clothes," said Joanne.

"Hell no, you're trying to get me to look ridiculous at my advanced age," commented Charlie.

"You could put on a beard and pretend that you're the "old geezer" that was in the bank."

"Yeah, that would be smart, the next thing you know I'd be arrested for stealing the money," answered Charlie.

Suddenly, Joanne asked seriously, "Do you think the "old geezer" has really stolen the money? How could a man of his apparent age be able to handle all those heavy bags? It doesn't seem logical to me."

"I don't know and I'll tell you this, I don't want to get mixed up in it."

During their walk, the couple noticed the squirrels scampering up and down the trees, and as the couple circled around the huge lake, they could imagine an Indian coming around the bend in a canoe. It was a pristine lake and the trees grew so close to the edge of the water that the branches dipped down as if to take a drink.

"Isn't the lake a gorgeous sight this time of evening?" said Joanne.

"This is the time of day that I really love. The pressures of the day seem to take a short nap so I can catch my breath. Peace comes over me, completely blanketing the fears and worries that build up all day long. At home in all the confusion of the city, I rarely get a chance to recharge my batteries, but here God seems to mellow everything with a wave of his hand."

"Charlie, I think this place has affected you. For the last couple of days you seemed agitated and a little on edge. But tonight I think your inner self has shown itself at last—I like your inner self a lot."

"Well, thank you, Joanne. My wife used to say that if people got to know me better, they'd like me. But you're likable immediately!"

"Come on," interrupted Joanne, fearful that too many personal things might be said too soon. "Let's walk all the way around the lake."

"Okay, you lead the way," said Charlie as he reached for her hand. It had been years since he had held a woman's hand. Joanne must have felt the same way, for she giggled as she squeezed his hand.

Each step that the couple took, as they walked along the edge of the water was a step into a mythological forest. The moon sparkled through the trees and lit up the rippling waves. The surrounding darkness made the couple snuggle closer every moment. It appeared to Joanne that nature had deliberately sculptured this environment for young lovers. But then, a question entered her mind, "Why does it always have to apply to the young? Why isn't it just as viable for matured lovers or even elderly ones?" She looked up at Charlie, as if she was awaiting an answer. She quickly realized that for an older man he was positively handsome, especially in the moonlight. In order to cover up the emotional expression on her face, she tried to start a conversation. "Charlie," she said, "has there ever been a time in your life when the future was so uncertain that you were afraid to go to sleep at night? I mean a time when your faith and logic couldn't overcome the fear that filled your entire mind? Or when there appeared to be no possible way out of a bad situation?"

"Oh, hell yes! Today almost qualifies as one of those times for me," answered Charlie with a puzzled look on his face. "Why do you ask?"

"I didn't think you had a lot of problems. You don't appear to be suffering from any great decision that you must make right now. But then, I don't mean to butt into your life in any possible way."

"Oh, you know, there is always something in life that causes us anxiety, and there are times when one really doesn't want to talk about it," replied Charlie.

"Please excuse me, Charlie, I had no intentions of discussing our problems. And I most certainly would never ask you to divulge anything that you didn't wish to," countered Joanne.

Charlie grunted, "Well, maybe some day—"

For the next minute or two, the silence was only broken by the sound of small waves lapping on the shore. Joanne tried to change the subject once again. "Do you have any desire to move up here permanently since you are now alone?"

"No, I don't think so. I can't get used to the idea of spending the last days of my life here in the mountains, especially since I don't have many friends here. And I have no golfing partners. Since my wife's gone, I really haven't been able to put together a scenario that would allow me to spend my last days in an acceptable and honorable manner. The fear of death that many people have has never entered my mind. But the fear of living alone does frighten me. You see, I believe that when we die we merely give up our bodies, but our souls and all the information that was contained in our minds will continue to exist. We become weightless as if we were in outer space and we're invisible to everyone except those who are in the same state. When I pass on, I will become an invisible wisp of smoke that can only be seen by another invisible wisp of smoke. The nearest thing that comes to my mind is that I shall be like a cool summer breeze that glides gently over the countryside. One can feel the presence of the breeze but one can't see it or hold it. In fact we, as humans, can never be sure that anything exists after death, for we must depend on sight or touch for verification."

"I know what you mean, I always felt that if we go to heaven, it is like falling in love," joined Joanne. "There is nothing tangible, only feelings."

"You're right, after we pass on, I think we slip into a euphoric state that can't be understood or hardly even imagined. It is very difficult to describe or explain but it seems to be a feeling that is only good and pure. Instead of maintaining human form, we become only our mental knowledge and soul with no room for hate, vengeance, or jealousy. We are only knowledge. There isn't anything else. You can't see or hear or touch us. That's one reason why I am willing to pass over at any time for I feel that my knowledge and soul will meet with my wife's invisible wisp of smoke once again, and that is—heaven!"

The conversation made Joanne meditate about the various theories of the image of heaven. Then, gradually, both Joanne and Charlie turned their thoughts to the present surroundings, the beautiful pristine lake and forest.

At last, Joanne spoke out, "Maybe we're in the middle of heaven right now. Here we are, a man and a woman in the middle of this heavenly garden. Could anything be much better?"

"I think you're right."

Thoughtfully, the two made their way though the garden back to the car. The evening passed quickly as they drove home. They barely spoke. When they arrived in the driveway, Charlie said, "You know, Joanne, I leave my time-share tomorrow. I can't put it off any longer. I have to get out."

"Yes, of course, so why don't you check out in the morning and bring your clothes over here, and use my guest room? Then, we'll both go to Pioneer Day. I think the parade starts at noon."

"That's fine. I won't stay more than a couple of days. I've got to finish a little business before I head home." Then Charlie said, "You know, Joanne, as I think about heaven and passing on to the other side, I'm always reminded of the words of Ogden Nash:

> *How confusing the beams from memory's lamps are.*
> *One day a bachelor, the next a grampa,*
> *What is the secret of the trick?*
> *How did I get so old so quick?"*

Since I am now eighty years old, I would like to add:

*"Lord, couldn't you wait a little while?*
*I'm not ready to walk that very last mile.*
*When my passion for life is finally over,*
*I'll come as if walking through clover."*

*Signed,*
*Charlie Carson*

# Twelve

As he picked up the phone, the sheriff of Crystal Springs heard a familiar voice say, "Sheriff Macklin, this is Sheriff Jeffery over in Falon, North Carolina. We might have a break in your robbery over there. We picked up a young kid who has some information about the theft. He seems anxious to make a deal. He claims he'll turn over all the others who were involved. Let me tell you the way we caught him first. It seems that a very large young man stopped into a local bar in Falon. He is a good-looking boy with blond hair and a sharp pointed chin. He must be about six-feet-three and weighs at least two hundred pounds. As the boy strolled into the bar, Mel, the bartender, who's a friend of mine, gave him a slight nod and a half of a salute, because Mel had seen this guy before. At first, the boy behaved very well. He ordered a whiskey with a beer chaser and sat there quietly enjoying his drink."

Sheriff Jeffers continued his story, "The tavern is a typical smoke-filled pool room, where many of the local workers spend their time after working hours. The boy soon ordered a second and then a third. Within a few minutes, he was beginning to feel his drinks as he began a conversation with Mel. Gradually, he became more and more obnoxious. In a very loud voice, the boy began complaining about the rotten luck he had. He was blaming some old man for having ripped him off. At this point, Mel, the bartender, became interested," the sheriff continued, "so Mel asked the boy to tell him the whole story. Mel became suspicious because he had read in the newspaper about the theory of the "old geezer" ripping off the robbers after the theft. Mel kept plying the boy with drinks as long as he continued telling his story. The boy told Mel a cock-and-bull story about his father leaving him an awful lot of money when he died last week and his father had put it in a safe place where the boy could pick it up."

"Well, goddamn," the boy said. "By the time I went to the trailer park on the other side of Falon Mountain where my father said he left it, the money was gone. The only one who saw anything was old Mrs. Bryson and she told me there was an old man messin' around our trailer all morning so he must have found the dough and ran off with it. If I ever catch that son-of-a-bitch, I'll tear his balls off." After quoting the boy, the sheriff resumed the story, "Mel began to press the young man about the area where his father was supposed to have hidden his inheritance, and before long the young man admitted that the money wasn't hidden in a trailer but in reality was in a barn. Mel kept the pressure on until the boy admitted his father didn't live on the other side of Falon Mountain."

At last, the boy couldn't take the questioning any more, so he blew his top. "It's none of your goddamn business where the dough was hidden or where my pop lived. Stay the hell out of my business or I'll break your goddamn back! Shut your friggin' mouth and pour me another drink," he demanded.

The sheriff continued his story, "His attitude grew rapidly worse until he was challenging all the customers in the bar. All of a sudden, he flung his enormous body on top of a young man who had just walked behind him. Pretty soon there was a real donnybrook in the bar. Chairs, tables, glasses bottles, and everything that wasn't tied down was thrown. Mel got right on the phone and dialed 911. Within moments, the local police and the fire department were there to break up the fight. The cops hauled the boy to his feet, handcuffed and led him to the patrol wagon. They tried to sober him up at the jail with hot coffee and something to eat. But after being asleep off and on, he finally became coherent enough to answer some questions."

"I questioned him for hours and at last, he agreed to talk to you if we could agree to go easy on the charges against him," said the sheriff. "He said that he'd give the names of his two partners. So, Sheriff Macklin, please come over here and take this guy off my hands. I've had enough of him and maybe this will be a breakthrough for you."

"You bet," answered Sheriff Macklin, "I'll leave right away, and besides, it'll give me a chance to get away from these FBI bastards. They're worse than having your mother-in-law coming to live with you. They expect me to keep them abreast of all information and everything that I'm doing and what do I get in return—the shaft. They've become a real pain in the ass."

"I know what you mean. I'll expect you in about an hour." But it didn't take Macklin that long to master the twisting roads. As he entered the police station in Falon, he said hello to all the deputies as well as the other employees, for he had known all of them for years. Without any hesitation, he walked directly into Sheriff Jeffery's office and said, "Hello, Sheriff, it sure is good to see you again, it's been a hell of a long time. Where you holding this bastard?"

"Come on, I'll take you." The two sheriffs walked through the various corridors until they arrived at a cell in which the young man lay sprawled out on his bunk. "He's all yours, Mac. Now listen to me, young fella," Sheriff Jefferys said to the boy, "this is your only chance, so don't blow it. Sheriff Macklin's word is good and if you can work a deal with him, he'll stand by you. So I'm telling you, don't blow it."

"What's your name, son?" asked Sheriff Macklin. The boy mumbled something incomprehensible while turning his head away from the two men.

"Now son, you better listen up. I need your name and I want your honest story right now. I'm getting old and I have no patience for people who won't work with me. So, give me your name and tell me everything that you know about the robbery." Once again the boy, mumbled something.

"Knock it off right now, or I'll just turn you over to my deputies!" the sheriff shouted. "Again, for the third time and last time, what's your name?"

"David O. Trent," the boy said reluctantly.

"That's better. Now tell me what you know about the robbery in Crystal Springs."

"If'n I tell you, will you go easy on me?" asked the boy.

"First, I want to know who you are running around with. Next, I want to know how you were involved in the robbery. Then, let's find out where you stashed all those money bags."

"I ain't gonna tell you 'til I'm sure you're gonna get me off."

"Cut the shit. I told you a lot depends on what you've got for me. You start. Then I'll let you know whether I believe you. By the way, have you ever heard of the Computer Gang? You know the gang that's been leaving their logo at each store that they rob?"

"Maybe," answered David.

"Start talkin'."

"Yeah, I heard of them. They're the ones who sign everything WWW-DotCOM, but I don't know much more than that. Man lay off, I don't—"

"That's enough," yelled the sheriff as he jumped up, "Bring in my deputies"

"Okay! Okay! I'll tell you," said David. Then, as if a dam had broken, David began to unload everything. "The WWW stands for Wimpy Wilber Woeber and the DOT stands for—"

"You, David O. Trent, but then who's COM?" the sheriff broke in.

"Well, he's not from around here. You probably wouldn't know him."

"I don't care whether I know him. I want to know his name."

"'His name is Chuck O'Malley, you know, COM. He's the one who set everything up."

"Do you mean he set up the robbery in Crystal Springs, or do you mean the store robberies in Falon?"

"Both," said David, as if he had some pride in the gang's accomplishments.

"Both? Maybe you better tell me about the Crystal Springs heist first."

"We held up the bank," said David, "and took the money and threw it in the truck and drove out to Owens barn. We hid the bags under the hay. Then we drove out of there in Chuck's car and hid out in Falon for the whole night. The next day Chuck went back to the barn over the back roads after the road blocks were lifted. But when he got there, the money was gone. He was so pissed off that he threw a match into the hay. Well, hell, you know what happened then. That old barn went up like a fountain of flame. Some sight!" said David. Sheriff Macklin sat quietly for a moment contemplating what he had just heard.

"David, do you know where those two buddies of yours are staying?"

"I know where Wimpy lives."

"You mean Wilbur Woeber?"

"Yep, he's scared to leave his room right now. He's afraid to drive around in the red pick-up truck of his. He's scared that the old man that he was chasing the other day might turn him in to the sheriff. You know, he chased an old car the other day that looked just like the one that was parked near the back of the bank the day of the robbery."

"Chased?" said the sheriff.

"Yep, Wimpy chased a car a couple of days ago and he almost caught it, but the old bastard drove across the golf course, so Wimpy tried to cut him off but Wimpy got stuck in a wet spot on the third fairway."

"Well, never mind that. Where's Wimpy now?"

"In his room over near Mineral City, but I don't know where Chuck is, but Wimpy knows." David said quickly.

"Now listen, David," said the sheriff, "who knows that the police picked you up last night?"

"Let's see, Mel, the barkeep, and maybe some of the guys in the bar, but nobody else." David answered.

"You didn't call anyone, a friend or a family member?" asked Sheriff Macklin. David shook his head no. "Okay, then let's try something. I'll help you get out of this mess if you'll do exactly what I tell you to do."

"Promise?" said David.

"Absolutely. Now here is what I want you to do. You call Wimpy on the phone and tell him you've found some of the money. Now understand, you have to act excited, and then you tell him to call Chuck so they can both meet you at one o'clock at the front entrance of the old vacant grammar school on Lake Arrowhead. You know where that is? On the dead-end street called Pine Street. You know?"

"Yeah, yeah. I know. Both Wimpy and I went to school there, but I don't think Chuck knows. Like I said before, he's not from around here." David said.

"Tell Wimpy, you'll meet both of them there and that you can split up the money right away. I'll have Joe and Frank, deputies from this precinct, go with you to help make your phone call, and you had better make it sound really good or I won't get you out of this mess," said the sheriff. "In the meantime, I'm going to set up a trap at the school. I want at least six deputies with plenty of firepower hidden in the abandoned school and I want them there long before one o'clock. Now get going and make that call good—no mistakes or you're cooked." Then Sheriff Macklin turned toward David and said in a very low voice, "If you tip off your friends in any way, I'll see to it that you'll spend the rest of your life in jail. No shit."

"Sheriff Jeffery," Macklin continued, "I could use your help. I need a quiet room with a telephone, a tape recorder, and I need you as a witness."

"Sure, hell yes," agreed the sheriff from Falon.

Within minutes, David was told exactly what he was to say to his friend, Wimpy, with the two deputies and Sheriff Jeffery watching over David. Wimpy's telephone was dialed.

"Wimpy, this is Dave, Guess what?" he said enthusiastically, "I found it, all of it. No, I mean the money, all of it. I followed the old man that you chased and he lead me right to it. He stashed it in our old school down by the lake. Yeah, the grammar school, the empty one."

Knowing that the two deputies were listening to every inflection of his voice, David continued his act. "Yeah, I found it in the old kindergarten room behind the blackboard. Look I'll tell you all about it when I see you. Meet me at the front door at 1 P.M. and listen, bring Chuck with you. We've got to divvy up the dough and get the hell out of here." After a slight pause, Dave continued, "No, I don't have his telephone number. Don't you remember? He wrote it on the eye shade in your pick-up? Yeah bring him, we can't double cross him now. No, I'm not in Crystal Springs now. I'll be at the school at 1 P.M., okay. See you then."

David put down the phone and turned to the sheriff, "Well, was I okay? Wimpy's not too smart. He won't suspect anything. I'm sure he'll show up, but I'm not sure about Chuck. Chuck doesn't trust anyone. Anyway, you'll know Wimpy by the red pick-up truck that he drives."

"Good work. You really sounded very convincing," said Sheriff Jeffery.

By twelve o'clock, with David in custody, Sheriff Macklin briefly surveyed the area around the vacant school to make sure there were no cop cars in sight. The school was located at the end of a cul-de-sac with only one road in or out. The old road was partially overgrown with lush foliage and the abandoned school had most of its windows broken by the very accurate aim of rock-throwing children.

The deputies were well hidden in the school and near the front door. "Hey Chris," asked the sheriff, as he turned to one of his deputies, "Where does that road go that branches off of this school road?"

"Do you mean that one back there? It goes miles back into the mountains. We'll lose him if heads that way. Should I set up a roadblock about a half mile down that road?" asked Chris.

"Yeah, but make sure you're far enough so no one can see you from the branch-off," confirmed Sheriff Macklin.

"Mac, there's only one little dirt road that branches off the road where I'll set up and that one circles around Pine Hill and winds up back here where you are. There's no other way out once you're on that road."

"Okay, let's go. Everyone take your positions," ordered the sheriff.

Time passed slowly until at last the red pick-up truck entered the school road. It was moving slowly, almost stopping from time to time.

"Dave, step out the front door and wave him in. Don't blow it now." Sheriff Macklin cautioned.

David stepped out of the building and motioned the driver to pull the truck up to the front. But, at the last moment, David realized that there was only one person in the truck. "Where's Chuck?"

"He's coming. You know him—he's always suspicious so he wanted me to go first in case there's something wrong," answered Wimpy as he jumped out of the truck.

The sheriff quietly called from behind the school door, "Wimpy, you and Dave come in the door. You're covered by several rifles. Don't make a sound or a suspicious move. Just walk in."

Wimpy obeyed like a well-trained hunting dog, as Sheriff Macklin noticed a second car halt at the branch in the road. Then, as if fired by rockets, it sped onto the branch toward the mountains. Immediately, Macklin got on his walkie-talkie to yell to Chris, "He's heading your way, Chris. Be ready! Take him down if you have to."

Then just as suddenly, the car must have seen the roadblock, for it swerved onto the tiny dirt road that circled Pine Hill.

"Mac," screamed Chris into his walkie-talkie, "he took the little road—he's coming back to you."

With unbelievable speed, Macklin had his men closing off both ends of the tiny road, and when the driver found himself faced by a battery of rifles, he quickly gave himself up. "Step out with your hands up. I guess you didn't know where that road went," said the sheriff. "Careful, we don't want anyone shot. What's your name, son? Are you Charles O'Malley?"

"You lucky bastards. It's just dumb luck you caught me. Yeah, I'm Chuck O'Malley. Who else would it be?" answered the young man behind the steering wheel.

The entire sheriff's team was euphoric as they returned to their temporary headquarters at the Trolley Station. But now, they knew that their work would head in another direction. The capture was one thing. Now, they must interrogate the three thieves and put together a viable story. But more importantly, no one knew where the money was still hidden.

For hours the deputies took turns asking all kinds of questions and keeping the pressure on the young captives. However, the best story that evolved was almost identical to the one that the sheriff had originally envisioned. The three crooks had caught the armored truck guards outside of their truck and then they entered the bank, frightening the tellers with all kinds of fire-arms into giving up all the cash they had. When they ran from the bank, an old man attempted to interfere with their plans so they knocked him to the floor. They, then drove to Owens' barn where they hid the truck overnight, expecting to take the money the next day. The next morning, after the road blocks were lifted, their leader, Chuck O'Mally, came back to the barn to find out that someone had stolen their bounty and the rain had washed away all tire tracks. That's when he set the fire. All three young crooks were convinced that only one person could possibly have taken the money. It had to be the "old geezer" from the bank.

So now, the sheriff's highest priority would be to capture the "old geezer." But the sheriff did not know who he could be. With desperation, he had picked up the old mountain man called Franklin Delano Roose, even though he was sure that Franklin knew little or nothing about the theft. Sheriff Macklin questioned him by the hour. But it was difficult to pin him down as to where he was, for he rarely answered the question concisely. Instead, he answered, "I walked the path of the honorable, down the lane of loneliness to my heaven here on earth."

"Now, Franklin, you get around these mountains and you seem to know everything that's going on. So I want you to let me know anything that you hear or see. Now, you know I'm going to keep you overnight here so you can sober up."

"Well, Sur, you know I'd rather go home, I don't choose to run." His quotes were never accurate but always applied to his own situation.

"Who was that from?" asked the sheriff. "Coolidge?"

"Yas suh."

# Thirteen

The next morning was clear and cool. It was a perfect day for Pioneer Day in Crystal Springs. It was the kind of a day that people cherish, for it gives hope that everything is going to be better. It makes people feel that they are glad to be alive. Pioneer Day produces many outdoor events that are held for the children, as well as for the grown-ups who wish to display their crafts in open booths or tents. Charlie arose bright and early. He quickly packed all of his clothes and checked out of his time-share condo. When he passed Johnny's Restaurant on his way to Joanne's home, he noticed a line of people going in the door waiting to have breakfast.

Charlie loved the old lumber trail that he had to take to arrive at Joanne's house, and he had a very warm sensation when he drove into her short driveway, for there she was sitting patiently on the porch. She looked great with her endearing smile that seemed to say, "Welcome Charlie! I'm glad you've come, now let's have some breakfast together."

Charlie had hardly had his first sip of coffee when Joanne announced that Pioneer Day was the biggest day of the year in Crystal Springs and that it had become the most enjoyable for her. She explained to Charlie that she loved the various events, but more importantly, the innumerable crafts fascinated her. "Charlie," she said, "I know you'll like the contests—ax hurling, log cutting with chain saws, cutting logs with a two-man saw, rail splitting, horse-shoe pitching, and I can't think of how many more. Then they have all the races for the children, and, for the teenage boys, they have the greased pole with a hundred-dollar bill nailed to the top. That one is fun to watch, for most of the boys only get about half way up. Of course, the most popular ones are those that the children enter—like the three-legged race and the rotten-egg throwing contest, which always end with at least one egg splattering someone's head. Naturally, they have a lot of mountain music and the kids clog. But first, there is a parade. It's really fun to see all of these mountain folks dressed as they used to a hundred years ago."

As soon as the couple had finished breakfast and cleaned up the dishes, they headed toward downtown to set up a pair of chairs in order to have an excellent view of the parade. Almost at once the parade started, with the Grand Marshall riding his beautiful white stallion at the head. Some of the old-timers in the area were dressed in original pioneer clothing and carried shotguns that were longer than present-day guns. Others came on swaybacked horses that looked like they had been alive since the first pioneer trekked through this lush forest.

The parade was longer than Charlie could imagine. Women enjoyed putting on long dresses and bonnets to look like they were in fashion with the clothes at the time of the pioneers. The men, too, looked their part. They came in all kinds of clothing—everything from leather mountain garb to suspenders and dungarees. At the end of the parade came a couple of hay wagons carrying happy, excited children.

The streets were lined with onlookers who clapped as every new group passed. There were even three bands from the surrounding towns. At times, some of the tunes they played were almost recognizable. The parade sported several of the big local men carrying axes. Next came the men who cut logs with a one-man saw, followed by the two-man saw teams, and behind them came women dressed in brightly colored gingham with a variety of bonnets. The last man in the parade was Franklin Delano Roose, carrying a sign, "Only the Lord knows where the treasures are hidden."

Charlie laughed when he saw Franklin and waved to him as if they had been long time friends.

Joanne and Charlie made their way into the large pasture where the main tent had been raised and they strolled from one booth to the next, enjoying the handiwork of the locals. In many small tents and booths watercolor and oil paintings, wood carvings of all kinds, wooden chairs, pottery, jewelry, were exhibited, and in others lots of clothing, cowboy hats, and even wigs and hair pieces were displayed.

After covering the majority of the booths, Charlie's feet began to hurt. "Joanne, would you mind if we sit over there in the big tent for awhile? We can listen to the music and watch the clogging. I'm getting worn out from all this walking," he said.

"I wondered how long you were going to last. I've been waiting for you to say something for quite a while," answered Joanne.

Charlie had really been enjoying himself looking at all the exhibits, and never once thinking about the robbery or the money. He admired the men who handled the axes and the saws and he had a good laugh at the kids struggling in their various races. After a restful half hour, Charlie was ready to go again.

"Look at that jewelry booth over there. Maybe I'll buy you a bracelet or a necklace or something. You can always use one more piece of jewelry, I'm sure," said Charlie.

"You don't have to buy me anything," she said.

"I know I don't, but I want to. You know, you're nearly as bossy as my wife used to be." Charlie hesitated for a moment, realizing that this was the first time he'd admitted to himself his wife was no longer with him. Then he continued, "Please let me give you something. As a remembrance."

"Okay," Joanne said, blushing with reluctance.

They approached a small tent where a man was showing some of his homemade settings. In a few minutes Joanne, with Charlie's help, picked out a lovely bracelet made with local garnets. It was nice, but not particularly expensive.

Joanne loved it and expressed her thanks over and over again. By now, she was literally hanging onto Charlie's arm, pulling him from one tent to the next. Finally, they arrived at a tent that had a large mirror on the entrance. As Charlie attempted to walk by the tent, Joanne grabbed him by his arm and pulled him in. Before Charlie knew what was happening, Joanne snatched a wig from a mannequin and slapped it on Charlie's head. When Charlie turned to face Joanne, the wig was slightly cocked on his head. The expression on Joanne's face forced Charlie to look at himself in the mirror. It was obvious to both of them that they were looking at a replica of the "old geezer" in the bank. Immediately, Charlie snatched the wig from his head and as he turned back toward Joanne, she murmured, "I'm sorry Charlie, I'm really sorry."

There was a thick, heavy silence as Charlie scanned the area in the hopes that no one else had seen him. Then Charlie, in order to break the silence, said, "Joanne, how about heading for home? I'm getting kind of tired."

"Yes, of course, lets go. I'll make some soup when we get home unless you want a big meal."

"No, I don't want a lot to eat, I'm just tired, that's all."

As they walked out of the fairgrounds, they could still hear music coming from the main tent. "This has been a most enjoyable day, Joanne, and I thank you for it. It's been a long time since I enjoyed a day like this. How nice life can be when we have nothing on our minds except enjoying the companionship of your friend."

"Yes," said Joanne, "I really don't need a lot of other things to satisfy me, just peace and quiet. I guess you'd have to add love and friendship, too. I've been happier these last few days than I have for the last couple of years."

As Charlie sipped his soup using his best possible manners, Joanne said quietly, "Charlie, I want to apologize for the wig episode."

"No, no. Don't even mention it. It's over and no one has been hurt. In fact, I don't believe that anyone even saw us. But please don't apply anything special to my embarrassment. It just shocked me for a moment."

Joanne nodded, then stood up to remove the soup plates from the table. As soon as the kitchen was tidied up, Joanne and Charlie retired to the rocking chairs on the porch.

"What are you going to do about your daughter? Are you going to help her financially?" inquired Charlie.

"I try to give her something a little extra from time to time. Lord knows she needs it. But it isn't enough for her to live on. I wish she'd find another man, but she says since her husband, Steve, died, she doesn't have any desire to meet someone new."

Charlie interrupted, "She's young yet. I'm sure that'll change over time. All of a sudden, she'll meet someone who lights her fire and she'll wonder why it took so long to happen. Give her a chance, she'll meet someone."

Finally, the conversation continued until Charlie and Joanne decided it was time for bed. They each headed for their respective rooms hesitatingly. Each were deep in their own thoughts.

As the night wore on, the moon was high in the sky and played hide-and-seek with the clouds. At last, Joanne, wide awake, got up to go to the bathroom, after which she walked out on the porch. She pushed the screen door open and held it so it wouldn't make any noise, for she didn't want to wake Charlie. Joanne's mind was reminiscing about the last few years of her marriage.

Those years had been happy ones, but since then the years had been boring. Nothing to do and nothing to look forward to. "Talk about humdrum," she said to herself, "It's been that way ever since he died. But today has been the best. What's happened? I'm too old and too settled to start something new. Why did he come along now?"

As Joanne reviewed her present circumstances, she was sure that Charlie had something to do with the robbery, how much she didn't know. But there had to be some connection. Her review included the fact that she was at least twelve years younger than Charlie and they had very little in common except their paths had crossed at this moment in time. She could not think of one damn thing that should encourage them to get together.

And yet, she felt just like a school girl with butterflies in her stomach when she saw him, and her face flushed when they looked into each other's eyes. She had been determined not to become involved with anyone ever again. Her desire was to help her daughter, for her daughter had no money to speak of. All Joanne had were her wonderful memories of her husband, and she didn't want to belittle those memories. There was no logical reason for her to become involved with this older man, and there were a million reasons for her to ignore any advancement that Charlie might initiate.

The sound of a squeaking door startled her out of her reverie. She glanced around at the screen door and there stood Charlie in his bathrobe.

"Joanne, I didn't know you were up. I was sneaking out here because I couldn't sleep. It's so bright out tonight. The moon is as full as I've ever seen it."

Joanne's face flushed, her stomach seemed to flip-flop, and she gripped the arm of her chair just as she did when her dentist began drilling. "Come on, Charlie, come sit down. That moon and the cool breeze are just perfect. I couldn't sleep either. Today was so enjoyable and so exciting that my adrenaline has kept me awake most of the night. Please, sit down."

Taking a deep breath, she blurted, "I've been sitting here thinking about my life and all that's happened. Then suddenly, you appear out of the woods and disrupt everything. Now, I'm really confused. My life was so solid and on track, but no more."

"Joanne, please don't talk about our lives. I didn't come here to disrupt your life or mine. Somehow, a lot of things have happened up here in North Carolina that have been unexpected and unusual. They have had a very profound effect on my life. I am trying to straighten 'em out with the least possible consequences and the least possible disruption to anyone. But first, I've got to make a couple of decisions. They involve my life and my conscience as well."

"You don't need to tell me your problems, but if I can help, I'd be glad to. And incidentally, I agree with your philosophy that some things should never be told. My problems are probably a little different than yours, anyway," said Joanne.

"Not all of them. We have some that seem to involve both of us. You have affected my life beyond my wildest dreams. I had no idea that a person could impact an old man's life as quickly as you have, Joanne. I never thought of becoming anything more than acquaintances, but tonight, I feel things that have been dormant for years. I'm not very eloquent when it comes to expressing my feelings. In fact, at this point, I'm really not sure what my feelings are. So please don't laugh at an old man, but you've suddenly become very important to me. I thought that other things were much more important, especially in my later years, but now I understand that money, plans, and obligations all must take a back seat to new friendships or new loves. That's part of my dilemma," replied Charlie.

"Charlie," said Joanne, "I'm not sure you know what you've done to me. I'm about ready to change my whole life just to be with you."

"No, that's wrong," said Charlie, "You can't change everything because of me. I don't have much time left. You know, I've had a quadruple bypass and the old ticker's not likely to last too much longer. The funny part of it is that nothing comes along in life when you're looking for it. My hope, right now, is that with any luck I'll be able to live out my life with no trouble or scandal and I'd like to leave my children with a decent inheritance. Of course, now there is one more thing added. One which I don't know how to handle and that's where you come in." Charlie continued, "I've had a great life. I've lived with passion like any normal person. And the Lord has been extremely good to me in a great many ways. Perhaps not spectacular, like being rich or famous, but great in other ways. I can't expect the Lord to come to my assistance with such a short time left. Even if I live a long time, I'll probably need help. I couldn't ask you to take a chance and end up a nursemaid. You need a straight and narrow path, not a series of crossroads. So Joanne, please don't expect that we can get together just to enjoy the last few moments of our lives. It isn't plausible. And right at the moment, it doesn't look possible."

"Look Charlie, there is one thing I'd never do," said Joanne. "I'll never force myself on you nor put you in a position where you'd feel an obligation to me. Never!"

"I don't feel that I must put my arms around you to show my feelings, and I don't feel that I must jump in bed to prove that you are the only one for me. I think, age has mellowed those desires or maybe, I see everything in a different light, not just sex. Perhaps, time has proven that the most important organ in the body is the brain, not those organs that seemed to control us when we were young." Charlie hesitated. He didn't wish to become too serious, so he switched his emphasis toward the humorous side. "Wouldn't the kids have a good laugh at me? I can just hear 'em. They'd be saying, 'Hey old man, what are you thinkin'? You're acting like a teenager. You're talkin' sex with a much younger woman. Hey Dad, remember, there's no fool like an old fool.'" Charlie continued, "That old cliche really fits me, doesn't it?"

"It's really quite funny for two older people to sit here giving excuses to one and other as to why they're having feelings toward each other." Joanne said, "Wouldn't it be wiser just to accept what life has dealt us and enjoy it?"

"You're right, Joanne, but in the meantime, we don't want to hurt anybody, especially ourselves. You and me, that's what is important at this stage." Charlie was silent for a moment, then said, "Here we sit in the middle of the night, professing our love for each other. We really haven't gotten to know each other except for the last few days, under very odd circumstances. Our love life might be in jeopardy due to the disparity of our ages. And in spite of my age, I feel a little embarrassed by the whole affair. Of course, I'm speaking for myself when I say that I'm not sure my performance would measure up. Especially, since you are much nearer the prime of life and you might feel that I'm, well, frankly, just a little over the hill."

"Charlie, please don't go on with that thought," said Joanne, "I think that both of us ought to have our brains analyzed. Are we nuts? There are so many things against us that we ought to wait until some of our problems are solved." She moved gracefully from her rocker to the ottoman and planted herself right in front of Charlie. Her knees touched his which caused small shocks of electricity through both of them. "Charlie," she said, "I agree with most everything you've said, so let's not jump into some situation we can't sustain for an extended length of time. Let's pursue it like the two matured adults we are, in hopes that down the line, we can enjoy life together no matter how short it may be."

Charlie didn't answer. He just reached out to smooth Joanne's gray hair.

The tender touch was more than enough for Joanne. A lump formed in her throat and tears welled up in her eyes. She tried to speak but nothing coherent came out.

Finally, Charlie said, "I sure wish I was a few years younger."

"Oh, Charlie, I'm sure there's enough fuel in that old engine to climb any mountain in these woods. As a matter of fact, I could tell by the way the old engine started just now."

Charlie laughed, glad the conversation had become less serious; then he said, "Joanne, I'll make a deal with you. We'll give it a—"

"Nope! No deals!" she interrupted. "I warn you, be on your guard, I'm gonna do my best to make you feel as strongly as I do. So watch out, Charlie!"

"How do you know how I feel? Right now, I'm heading for bed, alone."

Joanne called the dog as she arose from her wicker rocking chair, "Come on, get up, Sapphire, it's time to go to bed, you've got to visit the woods before you can sleep." Sapphire struggled to his front feet and gradually leaned forward until he was balanced on all fours. After a long stretch, the big black-haired dog trotted towards the woods to take care of his business, but as he approached the small stream, his ears perked up and the hair on the back of his neck bristled. He stop to sniff the air. Then, with a low growl and a small bark, Sapphire quickly took care of his business and raced back to the house. "Well, what did you see out there, Sapphire? Was it a boogeyman or what?" asked Joanne

"That's a wonder-dog you've got there, Joanne," commented Charlie.

"Yes, I think so too. I feel very protected with him around. He is so big that strangers are afraid to approach the house, although in reality he is as gentle as a snuggle bunny." With that Sapphire curled up in his personal bed, which was next to the fireplace, while the two humans each headed to their respective rooms.

"Goodnight Charlie," called Joanne as she closed her bedroom door. It was only a matter of moments after each had turned out their lights when there was a loud noise coming from the logging road. Again and again, there was a metallic crash out near the road.

Charlie could hear Joanne's bedroom door open. So he crawled out of bed and opened his door. Joanne was standing at the front window with Sapphire next to her, looking out toward the dirt road. She turned toward Charlie to say, "Probably, some coons turning over my garbage cans. I'll have a mess to clean up out there tomorrow." At that moment, there was a very loud bang, as if something huge hit the cans.

"Boy, that sounds like something bigger than a coon," said Joanne. And again there was a noise that was louder than a coon could make. Charlie became aware of the rustling of some bushes that were close to the house. "Joanne, do you have a gun?"

"No! Not handy; I'm not sure I have any cartridges for my shotgun, anyway."

"Well, have you got anything that we can use as a weapon?"

"Why, what do you see?"

"Wait, listen! Sounds like something coming on your porch."

"Let me look," said Joanne, as she pushed toward the window.

Apparently, even Sapphire had become concerned. He let out several gruff barks that should have been enough to scare the most courageous mountain man, but then even he turned and ran into Joanne's bedroom. Charlie turned his head to see Sapphire dive under Joanne's bed.

"Hey, that brave dog of yours is hiding under the bed. He's no help. We need a weapon. Grab one of the fireplace pokers and I'll grab one. Which room can we be most safe in—what is it anyway?" asked Charlie.

Meanwhile, Joanne was peeking out another window, "It's a bear! A big black bear! We couldn't save ourselves with a fireplace poker."

Charlie's mind shifted into high gear. As he considered his options, he peeked out of the window so that he could confirm the fact that a bear was brazen enough to invade this house. It was obvious to Charlie that the large black bear could enter the house with a minimum effort, and that there wasn't any place to hide.

Joanne calmly looked around the living room and quietly spoke. "Oh, well, there is nothing in this house that is worth dying to defend, so if he comes in the front we'll just quietly walk out the back—bring your keys, we'll just drive away in our car." With that Joanne leashed Sapphire and they both moved to the back door. Charlie took up a sentry post so that he could see the front door and some of the windows.

As they waited for something more to happen, Charlie's mind focused on what Joanne had said. "If he comes in the front, we'll just walk out the back." It seemed so very simple. Why doesn't that apply to my dilemma? "While everyone is at my front why couldn't I walk out the back?" But Charlie's thoughts were suddenly interrupted by the smashing of a front window. The sudden noise scared everyone, Joanne, Sapphire, Charlie, and even the bear. The bear turned and ran down the steps of the porch and wandered off toward the small stream. The crisis appeared to be over for the moment. Joanne said, "I'll call the wildlife authorities tomorrow morning to warn them that there is a bear in the area. They'll handle it and they'll warn everyone in the area to be careful. That bear's gone for now, so I guess we might as well go back to bed."

After a short conversation about the whole episode, each headed to their respective beds once again. This time, they hoped, for the rest of the night. But there was one thought that kept tormenting Charlie as he lay in his bed. Maybe there is a possibility that Joanne might be interested in sharing the money and running away together. "It's a dumb idea, but it sure would be fun because Joanne and I seemed to be very compatible," thought Charlie.

# Fourteen

The smell of bacon caused Charlie to speed up his shaving in order to have that first satisfying cup of coffee, followed by eggs and bacon.

"Good morning, Joanne," Charlie said as he hurried to the breakfast table.

"Good morning, ah—darling," she said, hesitating slightly.

Charlie looked at Joanne as his brow wrinkled. "How'd you sleep, after we finally got to bed?"

"Perfectly, now that you know how I feel about you. What would you like to do today? How about church? Then after, let's go to Timber Lake for a picnic—just you and me."

"Great!" Charlie said.

It wasn't long before Charlie was carrying two chairs over the hill where the old inn had burned down a few years ago, down to the edge of a magnificent mountain lake. The mountain across the lake rose up out of the water like a huge bald-headed man. Solid stone was exposed halfway up and then a few straggly trees stood on the top. The lake wandered north for about two miles, and there the foliage took over. The peninsula, with thousands of trees, jutted into the water. There were no houses in view to mar the virgin forest around the water's edge.

A canoe or two went by the scenic spot that Joanne had picked out for their picnic. The food tasted better than normal due to the special surroundings. A cool breeze kept the bugs away from their expertly prepared lunch. Their conversation covered everything, both the past and the present. Once in a while, the future crept into their repartee, but neither party dwelled on that. It was the present that took center stage.

"I'm so appreciative that you invited me to use your guest room," said Charlie. "I'm not sure where I would have stayed otherwise. You know, I'll have to leave for home by Wednesday. The kids have been badgering me to come home. They think it's time for me to report to my daughter, Susan. She sort of runs things in our family, especially since my wife died. All three of you, my wife, my daughter, and you, seem to react to things in a similar manner. Each one of you reminds me of the others. You each know what you want and what's more important, and I think you all know how to get it."

Joanne talked about the problems young adults faced these days. From the struggle that single mothers have, to the problems that would evolve in their future. Charlie listened to Joanne talk, but he actually heard very little. His mind had become focused on his present problems, mainly what he should do with the money.

Charlie reviewed everything again in his mind—the money, that damned red truck, Bobby Dee's suspicion, Charlie's lack of a friendly ear that would listen to him, the danger of his children becoming suspicious, his conscience becoming stronger by the hour, the fear that the sheriff was getting closer day by day, and the flood of little annoyances that cropped up every day. Things such as supposing someone found the money, or how would he transfer the money to his children without the IRS sticking their noses into everything, keeping Joanne from becoming involved, and being unable to trust anyone. Now, he firmly believed that he should give the money back. But how can millions of dollars be returned without being caught or without involving anyone?

If he dropped it off somewhere for the police to find, even a policeman might be tempted to take the money. If he dropped it near the police station, someone might see him. If he called the police on the phone, then he'd have to trust the person that he told. He would have the same problem if he gave the money to someone to deliver it for him. On the other hand, could he trust someone like Bobby Dee to help him return it? It isn't likely, for Bobby Dee already admitted that he wasn't sure what he'd do if he had the money.

The afternoon slipped by until at last Joanne and Charlie headed for home. By the time they made it, the evening news was on television.

The first announcement about the robbery came from Sheriff Macklin, who told about the success of his interrogation of one of the robbers who had been arrested in Falon. The sheriff announced that the young robber had copped a plea by giving the names of his two partners and by aiding in their apprehension. Then the sheriff continued to say that all three crooks agreed that the money had been stolen from them and that it probably was the old man from the bank.

Charlie listened intently and felt that the jaws of justice were closing in on him. He was certainly glad to have had the experience, but now everything seemed to be going against him. He couldn't imagine how bad it would be if he were to be caught. He would be devastated, humiliated, and the last days of his life would be intolerable. It might even bring on another heart attack. In addition, there would be no contact with his children as they would probably disown him. And now there was Joanne to think about. Charlie thought that after his wife died he would no longer feel that kind of responsibility. But now, he felt it again. Joanne was involved even though she knew nothing. It was imperative in Charlie's mind that he give back the money—somehow. Charlie hoped that he might use Joanne's theory—"if they come in the front, we'll walk out the back."

As he mulled the various problems over in his mind, he felt the beginnings of a plan. Then, as the plan developed in his mind, Charlie announced to Joanne that he must go to Mountain City to finish some chores before he headed toward Florida. He said, "Do you need anything in Mountain City? Can I pick up anything for you while I'm there? I think it would be best to go Monday morning early, I don't want to leave it to the last minute. It'll probably take me all day."

"No, I don't think I need anything, but I did want to tell you that I have a dinner party tomorrow night with several girlfriends, and I'm sorry, men are not allowed."

# Fifteen

Morning came, and Charlie thought about going fishing with his friend, Jeff, but at the last moment he changed his mind. He was too uncomfortable to fish. He had too many problems confronting him. Charlie left Joanne's with his breakfast half eaten for his mind and his stomach seemed to be at odds with each other over the decision as to whether or not to return the fortune. He was weaving his way through the increased traffic when he noticed Bobby Dee waving at him from his favorite rocking chair on the porch of the real estate office.

"Come on over, Charlie," called Bobby Dee. "I wanted to call you but I didn't know where you were staying." Charlie stepped lively until he arrived at the foot of the steps to the porch, then mounted as if he had suddenly realized his age, which made him struggle to the top step.

"How have you been, Bobby Dee? You're looking good as you sit here surveying your town," observed Charlie. "What's new in the robbery? Did anyone turn themselves or the money over to the sheriff?"

"Gnaw! There hasn't been nothing new since yesterday," continued Bobby Dee. "Whatcha doin' tomorrow night? Momma and I are having an old-fashioned hoe-down out at the farm. We've got a lot of local friends and some kin commin' and o'course they'll bring their fiddles with 'em."

"That's very nice of you to invite me. You'll have to tell me how to get to your farm, I'm not sure that I know exactly how to find it," returned Charlie.

"First, we'll have a great spread. Then after we chow down, we'll all pickup our musical instruments and play a lot of real mountain music. We got Disher on the fiddle and Billy Ray on the banjo. O'course Ferman will bring his tubs and sometimes, Lottie will play the harmonica, if she has a mind to. The kids might clog when they ain't runnin behind the barn to giggle over the latest *Play Boy* magazines. So if you ain't doing much, come for the eats about 5:30 P.M. tomorrow."

"That's great, I'll look forward to it. What can I bring?" asked Charlie.

Bobby proceeded to tell Charlie exactly where to go through the backwoods, turning first here, then there, until one could see the old house sitting on top of a knoll covered by scraggly bushes as well as a few huge sprawling oaks and many rugged locust trees. It was obvious that the trees had been strategically planted by earlier generations, for they surrounded the house in a manner to form a barrier to the cold north winds. From the knoll, the pastures swept down and away until they met at the foot of the ancient tree-covered mountains, which rose up hundreds of feet on every side of the cozy little green valley.

Again, Charlie asked the question, "What can I bring? How about some wine?"

Bobby Dee laughed heartily, "No, Charlie, we'll have the best, sweetest shine that's ever been hatched in these here mountains. Cousin Jeremiah has a natural born talent for brewing that special shine, especially since he's been doing it for more'n sixty year. You come and I guarantee we'll show you one hell of a good evening."

The conversation soon shifted to the bank robbery as it normally would. Everyone was talking about this unusual current event, particularly in this small town of Crystal Springs. The conversation lacked any new developments since yesterday. So each participant seemed to rehash the same opinions that they had expressed the day before. At last, Charlie announced the he must go on his way, while verifying that he would attend the party at Bobby Dee's home that night. Charlie figured that this was a good evening to go, because Joanne had a previous engagement to visit her old girlfriends.

Finally, the time had arrived for him to dress for the evening party. Charlie was not accustomed to wearing blue jeans, but Bobby Dee had emphasized that he must come dressed like the locals for, if he didn't, they would probably stay clear of him. He felt as though he was putting on another disguise. "How many different pretexts must I use before this predicament is finally at an end?" he muttered to himself. With that he headed out the door to make his way to Bobby Dee's house. "Well, let's get on the road," thought Charlie. "Let's go see how the mountain people live. It must be vastly different than those in Florida and a far cry from those in a city like Atlanta. They certainly aren't as sophisticated as those city folks, but their intelligence seems to be just as great. Also, I think that they have a different type of intelligence, one which stems from nature. A sort of natural inherent brain power that seems to develop not from books or computers but from observation and good common sense. We used to call that 'street smarts' but instead I believe that it's more intrinsically bred. Since they live in the country, their thinking is molded by the problems that the woods, mountains, farms, and streams offer. They have the ability to survive all manner of difficulties such as storms, famine, poverty, and many other forms of turmoil. Plus the fact, these mountain folks can repair the most complicated farm equipment or automobiles as if they graduated from an engineering school. I don't think they are street smart, but they are certainly jungle smart. To me, these people are not dependent on the outside world. Perhaps that is a better mode of life than most of us practice." By this time, Charlie was turning his car onto the dirt drive that curled to the knob on which Bobby Dee's home was located. "Absolutely beautiful," thought Charlie, "I wonder if these country people appreciate this magnificent scenery—with the lush green valleys and the dark foliage-covered mountains that seem to bolt upright from the bottom of the valley. I also wonder whether they are really happy, or are their smiles merely a cunning masquerade?"

The drive up to the house seemed very long, for Charlie slowed down every time he saw another pothole in the gravel driveway. The house was built a long time ago with a wide porch running across the entire front. The shingle shakes on the roof were mildew- and mold-encrusted and looked like they had not been touched in at least twenty years. The clapboard had turned a soft gray and the dormer windows were wide open in hopes of catching some of the cool mountain evening breezes that swept through the valley. Charlie pulled his car into the large parking area where there were several pick-up trucks parked. Of course, the largest and newest was Bobby Dee's. Charlie looked down the hill to see four or five kids shooting baskets down by the barn, and to his left up a rather sharp rise to the porch, where the grownups were milling around, deep in conversation. Naturally, in the middle of all the mountain people, sat Bobby Dee in his favorite rocking chair, just like the one in town at his office.

At first, Charlie thought that Bobby was the patriarch of the family, but with a second glance Charlie realized that an older woman, very stout and with a rather severe dour look on her face, was controlling the entire behavior of all her kin and neighbors. She had an air about her that was unmistakable. She was in complete charge and she knew it. As a matter of fact everyone else knew it too. She was not only the matriarch of the family, but of the entire valley as well.

"Come up here on the porch, Charlie. I want you to meet some of my kin and our neighbors," called out Bobby Dee. "Now this here is my cousin, Jeremiah," pointing to the tall thin rather gaunt-looking man who was dressed in worn dungarees and a typical blue plaid work shirt. "Why don't you get Charlie a mug of your famous shine?" Jeremiah continued to lean against the porch post until Charlie stepped up one step and extended his hand toward Jeremiah, who after a nod of his corrugated face, turned toward the kitchen in order to retrieve the drink for Charlie. "Don't mind old Jeremiah, he's going to look you over for a while before he'll decide whether he likes you or not." Bobby Dee continued with his introductions. "This here, standing behind me is Gramma Willis." He pointed back over his head to the matriarch of the family. "She is the cornerstone of our family, the one that keeps us all out of jail and keeps us talking to one another. But I warn you Charlie, you had better do as she says or you'll never be welcome in this family."

"Mrs. Willis," Charlie graciously acknowledged the introduction.

"Mr. Charlie Carson, wasn't it?" She asked in a very deep tenacious voice. One could tell instantly that she was determined to dominate the situation even though both Charlie and the matriarch were very close in age. Certainly, there was no graciousness or kindness in her voice or in her manner. "This is my oldest daughter, Maribelle." Turning toward her daughter, she gave her orders for the commencement of dinner. "Maribelle, why don't you and your sister start serving the dinner?"

"Awe, wait a minute," grumbled Bobby Dee, "Charlie hasn't even started his drink. Maribelle, why don't you take Charlie over there and introduce him to our neighbors, the Applebys?" Apparently, Maribelle was accustomed to this type of minor confrontation for it appeared that she had no intention of obeying either one. She turned to make conversation with her Aunt Ida. They laughed and giggled together until Bobby Dee shifted his position in his rocking chair.

Maribelle immediately took Charlie's hand. "I'm Maribelle, Bobby Dee's wife. Bobby seems to have forgotten that you and I haven't actually met as yet, but no matter, come with me. This is Ferman and Lottie Appleby. They live over there across the valley in that house just beyond our red barn." She pointed her long fingers toward a white bungalow at the base of the ascending mountain. Then turning back, she continued the introductions to some of the others. "This is my sister, Eloise, and my Aunt Ida, and Mat, Eloise's husband, is down near the barn, shooting basketball with the kids."

As Charlie glanced toward the barn, he could see that there was a resemblance between Bobby Dee and his brother Mathew Mark. With a slight bow, Charlie greeted most of the rest of the family. He was wondering whether he could remember all of their names when Bobby Dee interrupted. "Don't worry, you'll meet everyone before the day is over, Charlie. If you can't remember which name goes with which face, just say, hey you!"

Gradually, Charlie made his rounds to meet the Cowans and all of the children. However, he had no way of telling which child belonged to which parent. It was at this point that Gramma Willis interceded in the general conversation, "Mr. Carson, why don't you come over here and set down next to me and Aunt Ida. Are you married or single?"

Charlie's answer was quick and almost discourteous, for he caught the inference that Gramma Willis was making. "No, I'm not married. I just lost my wife a couple of months ago, and I have no intentions of changing my present status in any manner."

"You had better watch out," chimed in Eloise. "Between Aunt Ida and Gramma, you could be in for the battle of your life just to stay single. They both carry cupid's bow and arrows and have an aim that would challenge William Tell. Come sit with me. This is my husband, Mat and I think you know that he is Bobby Dee's younger brother?"

Charlie welcomed Mat to the porch as they both drew up a chair to form a circle. It made an easy format to carry on a confidential conversation. Immediately, Gramma Willis took the lead in steering the direction of the conversation. "Mathew, what have you heard about the robbery?"

"Nothing new, Gramma, they are still looking for that "old geezer." He seems to be the key to this whole thing," replied Mat. "These are times when I think Sheriff Macklin knows more than he is telling. In fact, one of the deputies told me that the sheriff is now checking the hair dressers in town 'cause he feels that the old geezer must have bought the wig somewhere around these parts!"

Eloise jumped up when Jeremiah finally came back with Charlie's moonshine. "Okay, I'll get things on the table now, 'cause it'll take about fifteen minutes." Charlie's first sip made him gasp slightly. "You're right, Bobby, that'll clear your head." His second sip allowed him to appreciate the smooth taste, which was slightly different from anything he had ever tasted before. "Boy, that's smooth," he commented.

Bobby Dee leaned toward Jeremiah, "Tell Charlie about the time you hid in a manure pile with all your freshly made whiskey while the revenooers broke up your still." Jeremiah put his head in the palm of his hand, chuckled quietly. But he never added a word to Bobby's story.

"Where's Ma?" asked Gramma Willis. "Bobby Dee, get off your hiney and bring your mamma here 'cause here comes her friend Judith Dobson." Everyone turned their heads toward the barn where an old abused red pick-up truck came to a halt amid a cloud of dust, and out stepped a rather matronly looking woman who walked with very quick, short steps that almost made her look as if she was running.

At last, Aunt Ida spoke up for the first time, "Don't pay her no mind, Mr. Carson. She's just out to get a new husband 'cause her man was killed in an accident last summer when the back-hoe fell over on him. Besides, she ain't got no sense of humor. I think a lady has got to cultivate a sense of humor like I have, don't you, Mr. Carson?" Charlie attempted to answer Aunt Ida but to no avail, for almost without hesitation Aunt Ida rambled on about how unsuited Judith would be for any available unattached male. The more she talked, the closer she moved toward Charlie, until her breathing almost forced her buxom breast to pin Charlie against the porch railing. It was very obvious to everyone that Aunt Ida had surveyed her prey and was now making a move to capture her target. She kept up a steady flow of babbling that followed no coherent direction until Charlie edged his way toward Mark and the other men.

Fortunately, the screen door flew open when a monstrous man bolted through the doorway. He was dressed in dirty farm clothes and his disheveled hair matched the gray stubble on his chin. He had certainly not shaved for several days and there could be bets made as to the last time that he had taken a shower. His appearance was overbearing and his manner was aggressive until he was confronted by the matriarch. One look from Gramma Willis told the brute that he had better clean up a little bit or he wouldn't be allowed at the table.

"My name is Jimmy Joe Jarrett. Some folks call me J. J. I'm distant kin to most of the folks here and I'ms the only one that does a day's work in the whole goddamn family," blurted the oversized mountain man as he stuck out his dirty bear claw to shake Charlie's hand. "Ain't it time to eat? I sho is hungry! I ain't had hardly a nibble since breakfast. Come on, Bobby Dee, drink up, let's eat so as we can get down to business."

Charlie's hand seemed to disappear in the grasp of the man who had a belly that hung over his belt like a plastic garbage bag filled with water. At almost the same moment, Judith mounted the steps to the porch and was immediately introduced by Bobby Dee.

"It's nice to meet you, Mr. Carson, I feel like I have met you before," noted Judith.

"Perhaps so, but unfortunately, I am not aware of when it might have been. Was it recently? You'll have to forgive an old man, for one's memory deteriorates with age," replied Charlie.

"Well, we actually didn't meet but I remember you on Pioneer Day, for I was working in the wig tent when Joanne Botts was teasing you by putting a horrible looking wig on your head," countered Judith. She continued, "anyway you didn't look like the "old geezer" who was in the bank when the bank was robbed. You're much better looking than that."

With a certain amount of embarrassment, Charlie was taken by surprise for he really thought that no one had seen Joanne and him fooling with the wig in front of the mirror. "Oh, do you know Joanne? I met her in High Prairie last year," retorted Charlie.

"Yes, I've known her since before she went to work in the High Prairie Bank. She's a very lovely lady. I wish that I could see more of her, but she seems to be very busy these days," commented Judith.

"Come on, everyone, time to eat!" yelled Ma, while she rang the large bell that hung near the entrance to the house. Then she walked over to the edge of the porch to wave to the children who were still shooting baskets down the hill near the barn door. It didn't take but an instant for the mob of children to race toward the dinner table. But even the kids couldn't beat J. J. to the table. He was already sitting with his knife and fork in his hands, with his hair wetted and plastered down. Everyone headed toward a seat that they had previously occupied. Aunt Ida reached out to grab Charlie's arm as she spoke in low voice, "You sit next to me, Charlie. Can I call you Charlie?"

"Yes, of course," was the obvious answer that Charlie gave as he adjusted the chair that Aunt Ida had chosen for herself. The sound of a spoon hitting a water glass was being repeated over and over again until everyone maintained silence. Charlie looked around the long table, silently counting the number of people. The children were all seated at a round table located in the next room within hearing distance of the grownups, and their behavior was exemplary.

At last, Gramma Willis stood up, expanding her bosom as if she were a peacock about to strut her stuff. "Let us now give thanks to the All Mighty. Why don't you lead the prayer, Ferman, since you're used to doing it at church?"

At once, the very tall, gaunt man arose from his chair with his head bowed to begin praying, "Thank you, Lord, for the food set before us this day and thank you, for the harmonious life that we share in this bountiful valley which has been blessed by your divine power. Through your saintly teachings, our families have learned the true meaning of life without animosity, jealousy, hate, or vengeance, and though we have little money, you have bestowed great wealth upon each one of us who were lucky enough to have been born under your guidance. Amen."

For a moment, Charlie thought that Ferman Few Appleby was going to continue with a long sermon, but with "Amen" everyone immediately began to fill their plates with food. Bowls of every kind of food were circling the table. Conversations broke out on every side of Charlie until it was difficult for him to hear anyone in particular. Charlie leaned back in his chair for a long moment to contemplate what he was observing here with these simple, unsophisticated people. They are happy, healthy, satisfied with their lot in life, and perhaps, most of all, they love and respect each other. Suddenly, his thoughts were shaken for he became conscious that something or someone was rubbing against his leg. He quickly responded by pulling his leg away only to feel a hand gently squeezing his knee. As he turned to look in the direction of the squeeze, it was obvious that Aunt Ida was making her move, for her head was leaning toward him more and more, until her head was almost resting on his shoulder. Charlie shifted in his seat until it became apparent, even to Aunt Ida, that her advances were not welcome. After considering the current problem for a short time, Charlie leaned closer to Aunt Ida to express his objections to her performance, "You know, Aunt Ida," he started to say. But Aunt Ida interrupted, "Just call me Ida, I don't want to be your aunt."

"You know," continued Charlie, "I'm almost eighty years old and I have recently lost my life's partner, and I'm long past my prime in every way, especially mentally. So, you see, I really don't need a new involvement with anyone. I have far too many other interests to waste any energy in attempting to recreate a relationship with a woman. My sex drive has diminished to a point that I am no longer interested in developing a man-woman relationship, can you understand that?"

At this point in the middle of the bountiful dinner, one member of this Willis family would jump to his or her feet to express a criticism of someone or something that had recently happened in the past few days. The only thing that was outlawed at this dinner was religion; no one was allowed to speak ill about religion, but everything else was considered fair game, even to the children. This appeared to be freedom of speech personified. However, if the attack was toward some member of the family, then all the other members became the supreme court of the valley and the accused was given a chance to defend himself. The majority would then render its decision and that was final. Most times the reason a person would rise from one's chair was to tell a funny story or joke or to tell of an interesting experience.

At one stage during this magnificent feast, the children became too loud and unruly. Without hesitation the leader of the clan, Gramma Willis, turned to Mark, saying, "Mark, you're the only one that can handle the kids and the only one that they will tolerate, so I think you had better pickup your meal and go straighten them out." Mark made no objections. He arose to join the children's table and within seconds stability took over.

"How did he accomplish that so quickly?" Charlie inquired. "He certainly has a knack for handling children. Perhaps it's because they love and respect him."

"Oh, yes," replied Aunt Ida, "we always turn to him to maintain order at that table." By this time giggling had replaced the unruly behavior in the other room. "You see that," commented Aunt Ida.

The food was as delicious as it was plentiful and the stories that the family told were funny and enjoyable. The dinner was an outstanding success. Everyone arose with a full stomach to retire to the comfortable chairs on the porch.

Now came the highlight of the evening, mountain music played by all local musicians. The first out the door was Bobby Disher, carrying his fiddle. Next was Billy Ray, tuning his banjo. Of course, Ferman was struggling to set up his tubs, which sound like a base violin. Lottie sat in the center of all these men with her harmonica laying in her lap. Then the one who seemed to take the lead and who played the guitar as well as sang all the country songs was a real country boy called Billy Bob Bryson who ran a small grocery store over near Lake Arrowhead. He was probably the most talented and seemed to help carry all the others so that they sounded very good. The other one who had a lot of talent was self-taught Bob Disher, who started the evening playing a tune that would excite everyone. "Orange Blossom Special" was surely a favorite with all members of the valley. Bob made the fiddle sound just like the whistle of a steam engine after which the tune was named. Within moments, the friends were all tapping their feet and clapping their hands in time with the country music.

One by one, the children joined in the clogging until their shoes stomping on the wooden porch floor resounded to almost drown out the music. Ferman, the gaunt lay-preacher, banged on the tubs so loudly that you would think he was attempting to overcome the sounds of the clogger's hoofs. What the little band of musicians lacked in perfect harmony they made up for in rhythm. You could hear Lottie make her harmonica moan and groan to add variety to country tunes, many of which Charlie had never heard before. At times J. J. would join Billy Bob in harmonizing in his inimitable style, which had a hillbilly's twang to it. The music continued for quite a long time, until Charlie noticed that Bobby Dee was whispering first to Jeremiah, then to J. J., both of whom immediately left the porch to enter the house. Bobby Dee turned to Charlie, leaned over, and spoke in a very low voice, "Charlie would you please come with me into the house? I must speak to you for a moment."

Charlie arose to follow Bobby Dee as the music kept on playing. They both entered a room in the back of the house which was used as a study. There sat J. J. with all of his massiveness and Jeremiah with his usual cup of shine in his hand. Bobby Dee seated himself behind the desk while he invited Charlie to take the comfortable winged chair in front of the desk. Then, without any explanation, Bobby Dee started the conversation. "Charlie, let me tell you about an opinion that the three of us have developed from a series of events and recent circumstances that have happened here in Crystal Springs. Our suspicions are that you, Charlie, are somehow involved in the robbery."

This absolutely took Charlie by surprise. His body jerked back into the chair and he verbally objected to the accusation. "Oh! No! No! No!" his voice trailed off.

"Now please, Charlie, bear with me for a few moments and then we will discuss this," interrupted Bobby Dee. "We want to help you and we think that once you have heard our proposal you will see the wisdom of it and then you will agree that you need us as much as we need you." Bobby Dee continued without giving Charlie a chance to say anything more. "J. J. brought this to our attention, and then upon analyzing all of the indications we could come to only one conclusion."

"First: You are the right size and the right age of the 'old geezer', who was present in the bank when it was robbed."

"Second: You were in the area the night of the robbery and I'm sure of that because I, personally, let you through the road block."

"Third: Sheriff Macklin has told me that he suspects that you know something. So he wants to question you."

"Fourth: You have a dirty old car that seems to fit the description of the 'old geezer's' car that had been parked behind the bank at the time of the robbery."

"Fifth: Jeremiah has seen you from time to time traveling the old logging trail, perhaps to and from Joanne Bott's home, but maybe there could be another reason for that."

"Sixth: Judith saw you with Joanne during Pioneer Day trying on an old wig and, although she says you didn't look exactly like the 'old geezer', she said that perhaps there was some degree of resemblance."

"Seventh: This is probably the most important—Jeremiah and J. J. were working their still a couple of days after the robbery when they saw someone running back and forth toward the old waterfall. They thought that it was the revenooers who were trying to find Jeremiah's still, so the two of them ran out of the area. Now, they suspect that you might have been hiding the money there. They couldn't see who it was because they were a long ways away. However, the person was about your size."

"Eighth: Charlie, you told me one day that someone had chased you in a red truck. Why? As a matter of fact, Sheriff Macklin told me that one of the robbers admitted that he had chased an old car like the one that was parked near the armored car during the robbery. Could that be yours?"

"Ninth: Old Franklin Delano Roose, who is somewhat of a clairvoyant, told me yesterday that he thinks you know more than you are telling anyone. I know he is usually right. Truthfully, he thinks you're the one who was in the bank the day of the robbery and he thinks you were trying to imitate him by wearing a beard. It seems that he has seen you messing around the area where Owens barn burned down."

By this time, Charlie couldn't take any more. He jumped to his feet to object to the accusations, but Bobby Dee's voice grew very much louder in order to dominate Charlie. "Now wait, Charlie, let me finish. We believe that one person alone couldn't pull this off all by himself. There are too many complications, too many problems, where could you hide the money for long periods, where could it be hidden so one could get to it quickly and easily, or supposin' the person were to get sick or even worse to die. Then what? Also, there is no one to corroborate any of your statements or give you an alibi. You need us to help you. To compound your problems, if you don't join us, we are giving you fair warning that we will search the entire area around the waterfall. So please be sensible, join us. We can work out a really good partnership that will benefit all of us. I want to reiterate we are convinced that you took the money and hid it near the waterfall."

Charlie started to get up but as he looked to his left, he became conscious that J. J. had also gotten up to stand next to him. He was very intimidating, so Charlie retreated to the safety of his chair. Fortunately, Bobby Dee waved J. J. off, then added, "Now listen, here is our proposition. We will give you a letter, signed by all three of us, stating exactly what we are proposing here, so that if anyone of us should double-cross you, then you will be able to take this letter to the sheriff to verify your story. Your trump card will be our signed confession. You can claim that we forced you into this situation. Then we can hide the money on our private property so that no one would be allowed to look for it. We have places on our property that we could hide a military tank and we can keep people from invading our privacy. In addition, it will always be handy to retrieve the money quickly and here, we're sure that no one can spy on us. We can, all four of us, funnel some of the money through various banks here in the mountains for the three of us are well known through out these parts. You will be able to go home without the fear that someone might find your treasure, only to have it stolen from you.

In case of your illness or death, your children will inherit your share under the same conditions. There is one thing that I'm sure you will agree is most important in a situation such as this, that you will have people on your team who can help you and people that will help you make the right decisions. People who can share your fears, doubts, and worries. Our plan is to divide the money, one half for you and one half to be divided equally among the three of us. As I said before, you will have a letter signed by the three of us and notarized, explaining that we have forced you into this agreement and that you had every intention of returning the money. Any additional requirement that you request will be given our best consideration. We do not want you to give us an answer now because we believe that if you go home to think about this in your solitude, that you will come to the realization that this is really the only logical answer. So we will expect your decision two days from now. Let's say at about this time at night so we can all meet here in this room after work. Charlie, I don't want to threaten you, but please don't try to grab the money and run, because you know that the sheriff is a good friend of mine and I'm sure he will believe me over you. So please join us, don't fight us!"

At last, Charlie stood up on very wobbly legs. He steadied himself by holding on to his chair. The scorn on his face expressed more than he could verbalize, but finally he mumbled, "Bobby Dee, you're wrong, dammit, I'm not involved in anything." Then his voice increased to a point that he was almost yelling, "No, I don't know anything about it!" Logically, Charlie knew that he could not show any crack in his mask as that would give him away and then he would no longer hold the high ground. "Let me get out of here, you bastards are nuts."

Bobby Dee ignored the outburst by commenting, "Now, Charlie, we expect you two evenings from now. I'm sure you will agree with us that there is no other way out of your predicament.

As a matter of fact, if you try to skip out with all that money, your new found girlfriend will be visited by the sheriff because Jeremiah has suggested that you must have confided in someone and she seems to be your only friend. So now, you have several people involved, your sons and your mistress."

Anger filled Charlie's brain. His fury forced him to stand up abruptly, lean over, and whisper into Bobby Dee's ear, "You bastard, if you involve any of them I promise you I'll blow your head off—and remember, I'm old enough so it won't matter to me if I have to burn in an electric chair." Then in a louder voice, one which the other two men could hear, "and that's a promise." Charlie eased his way toward the door, then with a last show of anger he yelled, "I know absolutely nothing, so do what you damn well please! As for your time limit, I'm not going to be here anyway. I'm going to my relatives in Mountain City." As Charlie slipped out the back door, his mind focused on his last statement. "Why did I say anything about not being here? I'm sure it made me look as though I was going to bend to their demands." He trotted down the hill and within seconds drove out of the valley, but he knew that he couldn't go back to Joanne's right away. He must take some time to gather his thoughts and to calm himself.

The more he thought of the evening's events, the more squeamish his stomach felt. "God, they know or at least they have guessed correctly. Hell, if they look in the area where they believe I hid the money, then they will surely find all of it. That goddamn Jeremiah. You might know he'd have a whisky-still there. Oh, that's silly; he isn't my problem. I just can't let this happen. I don't want any partners. Actually, I don't want the money either. It's nothing but trouble and it looks as if trouble is going to increase, especially with three partners. I don't mind Bobby Dee, but that oversized pig, J. J. and that air-head, Jeremiah. I guess I'm really trapped with no way out unless I give the money back. Well, those greedy bastards think I'm too old to fight back—Hell no! I feel young enough to give them one hell of a fight." Charlie hesitated a moment, then said to himself, "I guess I've been just as greedy as they are, so there is no alternative. I've got to give the money back. Unless—let me think about it—there must be another way."

Charlie was fuming with desperation and fear because he felt that this hillbilly triumvirate had maneuvered him into an untenable position. Every alternative seemed to finish at a dead end. As Charlie drove his car into Joanne's driveway, he could see her sitting on the front porch. Her presence's gave Charlie a strong feeling of stability. At her feet lay Sapphire, who picked up his head and ears with the approach of Charlie's car. Charlie quickly made his way to the porch with firm and determined steps.

"Well, you're home early. I didn't expect you for another couple of hours."

"I know, but something has come up that I must discuss with you."

"It must be serious," noticed Joanne, "'cause you look like you could bite my head off. I hope I haven't done anything to cause you—"

"No! No! Hell no!" Charlie answered, while hesitating to gather his thoughts. With his shoulders slumped and his head bent slightly forward, he began to speak. "Joanne, I had no intention of telling you about my serious problem, but Bobby Dee has forced me into making an immediate decision. Therefore—"

"Now, wait Charlie, I'm not sure you should tell me anything that you really don't want to. I'll bet it concerns the bank robbery, doesn't it? I really don't want to hear it."

"You're right, it is about the money. It is mandatory that I tell you the whole story now because I have no more time. I'm being forced to make a move. But before I do, I am proposing a plan that involves you." Charlie proceeded to tell Joanne the whole story. How he intended to rob the bank alone and how he stumbled in on an ongoing robbery. Then he explained how he stole the money and hid it near the waterfalls. The threats by Bobby Dee and his two cohorts and the pressure from the sheriff and the FBI made him realize that he must act at once. No more procrastination. It's now or never.

The two discussed the details of the whole story. Until, at last, Charlie made his proposal. "Joanne, you know that I am as old as Methusala and I'm sure that I do not have a long time on earth. However, I have come to the realization that in spite of my age, I have fallen in love with you. That sounds ridiculous, but it's true. I want you to marry me and together we will go to the waterfalls to pickup a the money. Then," said Charlie, "we will wrap up five packages of money. Somewhere around a million apiece. One for each of my children and a larger one for your daughter, and we shall send them to their respective homes in Florida. In the meantime, you and I will fly to South America to a country that has no extradition agreements with the U.S., with enough money to live on easy street for the rest of our lives. That would make me a very happy man, and I hope you would be too."

"By our leaving this country, the sheriff and FBI will be positive that we stole all the money for ourselves and they would have no cause to suspect that our children have benefited from our gifts. We would warn the children not to spend it carelessly and they would all enjoy a truly great legacy. They could come to visit us from time to time but of course, we could never come back to the U.S."

"Charlie, Charlie! You're a dreamer, I couldn't do that. It's dishonest and immoral. You and I have never lived that way and I doubt we could change now. We just couldn't make it work, besides we could never come back here again. I'm sure there is enough money to be worth the risk and I know that I love you enough to follow you anywhere, but this is too outrageous to seriously consider. No, Charlie, I couldn't do that. There must be another way to solve it."

"Yes, there is, and I have already decided what I shall do if you won't join me. The only viable alternative is for me to make a deal with the sheriff so that I'll get out of this relatively easily and then I shall turn the money over to him."

"Please don't turn it in unless the police promise not to charge you with anything more than a misdemeanor. You must understand, I can't do this."

"I understand. No, I won't turn in the money unless I have an air-tight deal, but I must settle it tomorrow." The rest of the evening was spent discussing the various alternatives, but the two adults finally went to bed, separately, with no change in Charlie's plans to go to the sheriff in the morning.

# Sixteen

When Joanne decided that she was tired and it was time for her to go to bed, they each proceeded to their respective bedrooms to attempt to sleep. The minute Charlie put his head on the pillow, he realized that his adrenaline was flowing through every vein. He tossed and turned for almost an hour without closing his eyes. He was angry at Bobby Dee for his threats and he was fearful that his conspiring plan to keep the money for himself was falling apart. At last, he sprang from his bed like a buoy popping to the surface when released from deep in the water. He threw on his clothing, grabbed his flashlight and slipped out of the house without disturbing Joanne. He hastened down the lumber trail toward the spot that he had entered the thick woods on his way to the waterfalls. His immediate plan, which he had not thought out well, was to grab as many bags of money and hide them near the edge of the road, so that early the next morning he could throw them into his car. Then, he could decide what he would do next, and at least, Bobby Dee wouldn't find the money buried near the waterfalls.

He entered the woods on the familiar path that led him directly to the old log that lay across the small stream. As he crossed the log, walking with one foot directly in front of the other and with a great deal of care, he thought he heard a rustle in the bushes behind him. But after a small hesitation, Charlie continued his trek. It was so dark that most of the time, Charlie had to use his flashlight in order to stay on his path. Again, he thought he heard someone behind him, but when he stopped there was no movement in any direction. Soon, he was struggling up the slippery wet hill toward the base of the waterfalls, when he heard the snapping of branches. He took two or three steps, then quickly stopped to listen. Now, he was sure someone was following him. He performed the same scenario once again, and again he heard the steps, and then immediately silence. A chill ran up his spine. He had no weapon to defend himself. Quickly, he moved forward to find a thick branch that he could use to hit the person who was following him. He actually ran a few steps to duck behind a large oak tree. Then, he waited. At first, there was no sound of feet rustling the fallen leaves but as he waited silently the sound started again. The one who made the leaves rustle was slowly approaching the tree that hid Charlie.

Charlie drew the stout piece of branch back as if he was about to hit a baseball when a huge hulk of a man stepped around the tree. Charlie started to swing but held back, at the last moment, for he recognized the barrel of a shotgun pointed directly at his chest. Then, he recognized the man behind the gun. It was J. J., the big fat slob that had confronted him in the back room at Bobby Dee's home.

"What the hell are you doing here, J. J.?"

"Ha, ha, I don't have to ask you what your doin, do I? Bobby Dee was right. He said you'd make a run for the money tonight. Now, drop that toothpick you're carrying or I'll blow you away."

"What the hell do you want with me?"

"At first, I thought you would lead me right to the treasure. But then, you had to hear me coming so now I'm going to ask y'all to lead the way to the money."

"Go to hell!" Charlie answered so quickly that it was really an admission that he did know where the money was buried.

"I'll ask you nicely one more time and then, if you don't lead me, I'll beat the shit outta you."

"You arrogant son of a bitch. What happens if I show you? Do you kill me, then?"

"You know I wouldn't do that—Bobby Dee made me promise that I'd bring you in alive, but he didn't say that I couldn't work you over a little bit. Now start walking!"

Charlie started to move straight back toward the log across the stream. For a moment or two J. J. tried to steer Charlie toward the waterfalls but he realized that Charlie was determined to head back toward the lumber trail. J. J. prodded Charlie with the end of his gun barrel several times until Charlie knew that J. J. wasn't going to back off. In fact, J. J. increased the jab each time, forcing Charlie to move faster. As they approached the log, J. J. anticipated that Charlie might attempt to free himself

"Listen, you bastard, you cross that log and then you lay down on the ground until I cross. Understand my meannin'? Remember, I've still got this gun pointed at your ass!"

"I hope you slip off that slippery log. You better watch your ass 'cause if I get a half a chance, I'm going to wrap that gun barrel around your stupid neck."

"If you try anything, you old fucking bastard, I'll break your back over my knee. I'm reminding you once more that we could make you disappear and nobody in the world would know or care. Now, keep going up that lumber trail till I tell you to cut into the woods."

After a short walk, J. J. poked Charlie in the ribs. "Go in there to the left and you'll find a narrow path leading up the mountain." Each step along the path seemed like an eternity as the two men snaked up the mountain. From time to time, Charlie made a slight motion as if he was going to make a break into the woods to make an escape. But J. J. was alert enough to poke Charlie in the ribs. At one point as the two rounded another bend, J. J. called out, "Comin' in! Look what I've got. I found it on the way to the waterfalls." Again J. J. prodded Charlie, pushing him toward the still.

"Where did you find him so early in the morning?" asked Jeremiah.

"He was on the way to the waterfalls where he has probably stashed all that lovely money. Bobby Dee told me to stake out that area 'cause he was sure that Charlie would try to get the money." The three men continued on the path until the still came into sight. Charlie stood silently admiring the "Rube Goldberg" contraption. There in front of him was a still nestled in the trees. A fire was burning under the very large metal vat which contained the mash. From the top a Horse's Head (an old fashion stove pipe) carries the steam into a big wooden barrel called a Thump Keg. Then this barrel is connected to a worm (copper-coiled piping through which the steam passes and cools thus condensing the steam into pure alcohol). At the end, there is a bucket which is used to dump the alcohol into bottles.

Charlie stood quietly surveying the entire area. The slope of the mountain was overgrown with heavy trunks of oak trees that formed a canopy over the tangled branches of laurel bushes. Abruptly, half way down this slope a tremendous slab of rock protruded from the ground forming a large-sized cave. Apparently, the moonshiners had cleared a small area in front of this cave in order to build their still. From the trash and cigarette butts it was obvious that this still had been here for many years. J. J. turned to Jeremiah to say, "Give us a drink. Me and this old man. We've been walking through the woods for quite a spell."

Obligingly, Jeremiah pickup two tin cups and dipped them into the bucket while saying, "It's kinda green yet, you know."

Charlie reluctantly accepted the drink although he would rather have water. Charlie took a small sip and it was so strong that it made his whole body shudder.

In the meantime, J. J. took a huge gulp after which he let out a loud burp. Charlie looked at him with disgust but before he could make a comment he noticed someone coming out of the cave. Charlie immediately recognized the man. It was Ferman Few, the preacher, who acknowledged Charlie's presence by nodding his head. He walked directly up to Charlie and with his face only an inch from Charlie's he said, "Mr. Carson, tell us where you have hidden the money. Lord help you if you don't, for the consequences will be very severe. As you must know by now, J. J. loves to persuade people to do as he wishes. He is brutally persuasive."

J. J. laughed so hard that his fat body jiggled all over. Then he added, "I suren wish Bobby Dee would let me persuade him my way but since he's so old, Bobby's afraid he'd die." With that J. J. swung his huge fist into Charlie's stomach, forcing Charlie to double up with pain. "There," said J. J., "I wanted you'ens to have a sample of my persuasion power."

In moments both Ferman and Jeremiah tied Charlie with a very heavy rope. "That's not good enough," said J. J., and reached down and tied Charlie's neck close to his knees so that he was in a fetal position. With his hands behind his back, Charlie couldn't move in any direction. Between the three men, they moved Charlie into the damp cave and left him lying on the cold wet dirt.

The aches and pains crept into Charlie's joints from the damp dirt floor. He was conscious of dripping water splashing in the mud and soaking his clothing. If he strained, he could hear the three men arguing about where Charlie had hidden the loot. Occasionally, J. J. would walk into the cave, kick Charlie in the body, and then ask, "Are you ready to tell us yet? You better hurry up 'cause Bobby Dee will be here soon and he won't be as gentle as I am."

All Charlie could do was to groan. The gag that J. J. had stuffed in Charlie's mouth prevented him from saying anything. Charlie knew that he was in trouble but his age made the situation desperate. The more that J. J. pressured and badgered him the more stubborn and determined Charlie became.

By this time, the sun had risen high in the clear blue sky. Charlie lay on his side, thinking to himself how much he had misjudged this gang, when he heard a commotion near the other side of the still. Several men were laughing and joking. This made Charlie even more uncomfortable because he realized that he was the subject of the humor.

From time to time, either Ferman or Jeremiah would visit him, urging him to give up where he had stashed the money. Then he would mumble though his gag, "You know you guys are killing me. At my age I can't survive much longer and then you'll have nothing." His pleas made no impression. But at last, Ferman said to Charlie on his last visit, "Bobby Dee has arrived. You probably heard him laughing just now. He's going to run things from now on." Bobby Dee strolled up to the entrance of the cave and greeted Charlie, "Well, old man you tried to pick up the money even after we warned you, didn't you? That wasn't very smart, but at your age we don't expect too much, do we?" Bobby Dee reached down to loosen the gag so Charlie could talk.

"Charlie, we offered you an excellent proposition but you didn't want that, did you? Now, I haven't much choice, either you tell me all your secrets or I'll be forced to turn you over to J. J. and I think you know what that means."

"Oh hell, Bobby, if you turn me over to J. J., you know that I'll die and then you'll never know anything about the money. I don't think you're that dumb and if I tell you now—you'll kill me."

"No, I'm still offering you the same proposition that I offered yesterday."

"Stick it! That's my answer once and for all!"

"Well now, I don't like that attitude, so let me add a little more pressure to your position. We're sure that you hid all that lovely money very near the waterfalls. So if the four of us make a big effort to search the area, I feel sure that we will find it. Therefore, we really don't need you at all."

Bobby Dee hesitated. He was waiting for Charlie to answer but Charlie clammed up. It was worthless to argue with Bobby. Bobby had all the cards and he was playing them one at a time.

Bobby started again, "I'll tell you what I'll do. The four of us have to deliver some of our special white lightning over near Falon. So we'll give you three or four hours to think it over and when we return you had better decide to join us or you know the consequences. You must realize that we could make you disappear and nobody would ever find your body. There are many spots here in these mountains that no one has ever explored, so it would be easy for us to dispose of anything." Bobby Dee tightened the gag and the four culprits loaded the bottles of white lightning in a couple of wheelbarrows and headed through the forest.

Charlie lay coiled up on the damp ground with his bruises hurting more all the time. It was obvious to Charlie that this gang had used this type of persuasion before because they never hit him on his face. Charlie tried to change his position but found that he had been trussed up so tightly that he couldn't move. The cold dampness crept into every joint until Charlie felt sure that under these conditions he wouldn't be able to last very long. It was time to decide whether to fight it out or perhaps, at last, tell them what they wanted to know. He knew that he really had very little to bargain with. So he had to hope that he could persuade them to spare his life. As he contemplated his options he thought he could hear someone humming a tune. It wasn't nearly time for the moonshiners to return.

As the humming continued, Charlie could hear someone pouring himself a drink into one of the tin cups. Charlie wiggled and groaned as loud as he could, until at last, he could see a bent-over form appear at the entrance of the cave. The form stood over Charlie and immediately Charlie recognized him. The minute that the stranger released the gag Charlie called his name, "Franklin, Franklin Delano Roose. Am I glad to see you!"

"Mr. Carson, what under the sun are you doing all tied up and lying in the dirt?"

"Call me, Charlie."

"Yas suh, what did you do to Bobby to wind up like this?"

"Nothing, help me get untied. I'll tell you all about it"

"No sur. Bobby Dee is a friend of mine for years so you musta done somethin'."

"Franklin, please believe me, I've done nothing—they want me to tell them where I hid the money from the bank robbery."

"Mr.—Ah—Charlie did you rob the bank?"

"Please believe me! I didn't rob the bank but I am involved. I'll tell you all about it if you'll untie me."

Franklin looked at Charlie laying on the ground. He stood for an extended time pulling on his beard as if he was debating all his options. "William Shakespeare said, 'There are small choices in rotten apples'." Then, reluctantly, he leaned down to untie Charlie. "Now that I untied you, you must abide by the rules."

"Okay." Charlie told Franklin about the suspicion that Bobby had that Charlie had hidden the money. But he didn't go into the fact that he had stolen the money from the bank robbers.

The vision of hidden money triggered Franklin's mind for he immediately cut off Charlie's story and began to talk about all that he had. "I am one of the richest men in these mountains. I don't need any money. I have a very dry cave up there and I have clothes and people give me food and most of all I have freedom. Freedom from a wife, freedom from family, freedom from work, freedom from worry, and freedom to live as I want to. Nobody bothers me except Sheriff Macklin once in a while. So I don't need all that money."

"Well, I guess I agree, but sometimes you could use money to get a good meal or a warm place in the winter when the snow flies. I agree with you the older we get, the less we need material things. I think friends become more important than anything else. And also trying to please people seems to occupy a large spot in my heart."

"I like that too, that's why I untied you."

The two old men sat together and sipped some of the diluted moonshine. Their conversation became more and more enjoyable the deeper they explored each other's philosophy. They were surprised how many ideas and opinions they shared. Even their likes and dislikes seemed to match. They had each found a friend, one which would last until the very end of time. Above all else, the two were identical in their desire for fairness and honesty, and they both abhorred violence such as what Bobby Dee had inflicted on Charlie.

"Someday, I'll have to inform the sheriff of Bobby's activities."

"Yes, you should, for I know the sheriff asked you to keep your eyes open while you wandered through these mountains. Perhaps, I can help there too."

Charlie continued to talk 'cause he hadn't had a conversation as interesting as this since coming to the mountains. "Even at eighty-years-old it is fun to gain a new friend. I wish we had met years ago, but now it's time for me to go on my way."

"Charlie, you see, you don't have the freedom that I have."

"You're right—but I feel obligated to get the money back to the rightful owners and I must do it my way. While we have been sitting here, I think I've come up with a new plan."

The two old men said goodbye, and Franklin headed toward his cave while Charlie returned to Joanne's house. Charlie knew he must call Joanne at her job for she must have been frantic when she awoke to find Charlie gone.

"Joanne, this is Charlie. I'll have to explain what happened this morning but I'm all right. I've called the sheriff and I'm going to see him this afternoon. I'm not sure how much I shall tell him but I'll decide between now and when I arrive at his office. If you should want me, I'll be at the sheriff's office in High Prairie."

# Seventeen

Charlie felt sure that he would have to face a severe interrogation by Sheriff Macklin. After the phone call to Joanne, he picked up the phone and dialed the sheriff's office in High Prairie. It was very frustrating trying to explain to one of the deputies that he wished to have a meeting with the sheriff. The officer on the phone kept insisting that he had no appointment and therefore, it was necessary to speak to one of the deputies first. At last, Charlie's patience ran out and he told the deputy, "I know who the 'old geezer' is, but I won't tell anybody but Sheriff Macklin, himself. So I'll be at his office in exactly one hour or I'll leave town and you'll never hear from me again."

Charlie had hit a nerve, for he could hear a commotion over the phone and several other phone extensions connecting to his line. Immediately, the attitude of the deputy became polite and condescending, "Yes sir. I'll make sure that the sheriff is here." Charlie hung up the phone at once so that no one could trace his call.

Within the hour, Charlie parked his car and walked quickly into the police station. A sergeant at the desk leaned forward, "Can I help you, sir?" Charlie hardly answered him about having an appointment with the sheriff when he was informed that there was a telephone call for him. "Sir, the party on the phone asked that you call her back immediately, for it is a matter of life and death. Here's the number."

Charlie looked bewildered but he dialed the number at once. Joanne answered on the first ring. "Hello, is this Charlie? Just listen, I'll talk since you are probably in the police station. Listen Charlie, I've changed my mind. I can't lose you now that I've just found you. I love you and I can't do without you. I'll go with you to South America or anywhere else. Wherever you say! Don't turn yourself or the money in. Please darling, we'll work it out,

together. I want to do this with you. For all we have left is that
we join together for as long as we have. Love will conquer all."

"Okay! I promise. I won't do anything."

Charlie hung up the phone and saw the sheriff waving him
to come into his office.

"Sir, my name is—" But Charlie never finished for the sheriff
interrupted him. "I know you, sir. You're the man who saved my
daughter. Your name is Charlie Carson."

"Well, I helped her when she needed someone. How is she
doing?"

The sheriff took over the conversation as was his usual
custom. "She is doing just fine. I've wanted to thank you for all
that you did but as you know, I haven't had a moment with this
robbery and the FBI hanging over me all the time. I haven't been
able to call you or to even think about anything personal. You
did a hellova good job that day at the accident. Now, Charlie, can
I call you, Charlie?"

"Sure."

"Before I ask you a few questions, let me point out some
facts, Charlie."

"First: this robbery is a major crime and therefore, when the
perpertrator is caught, he will face major consequences."

"Second: The FBI is now involved, and they are famous for
pursuing their suspects until they nail them, no matter how long
it takes."

"Third: The nation's media has grabbed a hold of this
robbery and they will be as tenacious getting the story as they
were when they were covering O. J. Simpson or Clinton and
Monica."

"Fourth, and perhaps the most important: I am determined
to clean this up for I have never allowed any loose ends in any
crime since I have been sheriff. So I can guarantee that I shall get
the culprit before I quit. However, let me say one thing more, I
am willing to make concessions, if I could solve this quickly and
if I could have the money returned safely. Please let's discuss this
situation and if you are involved, perhaps we can come to an
equitable compromise. I also hope that you will keep your eyes
and ears open while you are wondering around these
mountains. As you probably know, I have quite a few people

helping me, such as Franklin Delano Roose, for he has an innate talent for ferreting out things that happen in these mountains." The sheriff continued without even a hesitation, "What's this I hear that you might know something about the 'old geezer'?"

"I wish to apologize for misleading you but that was the only way that I could get passed your deputies. You certainly have a fortress built around you. The truth is, I don't believe I have any information that could help you. But I felt that I must come in and face you so that you won't suspect me in any way. If there is anything that you wish to know, I will be happy to answer all of your questions."

"Charlie, soon after the robbery someone said that they had seen a dirty old car in town that looked like the one that was seen behind the bank. Then Bobby Dee told me that you had an old car that matched that description. So then, I began to wonder whether you happened to be in or around the bank at the time of the robbery, and perhaps, you might have seen something."

Charlie had anticipated that question, so he was well prepared." Yes, my car was parked near the bank that morning. I was eating breakfast, or rather an early lunch, in Johnny's at the time, and of course, we all ran across the street when we heard the shots fired over near the bank. There were a whole bunch of us that ran toward the noise. I admit that I wasn't the first over there for these old knees don't react as well as they used to. But I got there soon after it happened."

"Do you know any of the people who ran across the street?"

"Gee, Sheriff, I don't know very many people in town, as you probably know I come from Florida, so I'm not acquainted with many except Bobby Dee and maybe the waitress in Johnny's. And it seems to me she came running over a little while after the rest of us. There was so much confusion around there that I really don't have much more that I clearly remember."

"What did you do then?"

"Well—let me think," Charlie hesitated, "I think I had an appointment in High Prairie. Yeah, that was it. I had to go to High Prairie and I never returned until it was getting dark and it was raining."

"Did you have to drive through the road block that we set up?"

"Yep, they let us through at the cliffs. And then they stopped us at the top of the hill on the way to Mineral City."

"Was that where Bobby Dee stopped you?"

"Yep."

The sheriff stroked his chin as he often did, and then spoke very slowly as if he was digesting all the information that he had heard. "You know that we aren't really after the 'old geezer.' But we think he knows where the money is hidden. We believe that if the old guy would turn the money in to our department then the charges could be reduced to—perhaps as low as a misdemeanor. After all, we believe that the 'old geezer' is in all probability at least eighty years old, so there isn't much sense in putting him in jail for the rest of his life. I'm sure that if I can talk to a certain judge that we can make some arrangements."

Charlie couldn't be sure whether Sheriff Macklin believed that Charlie was in reality the 'old geezer' or whether the sheriff believed that Charlie knew who the 'old geezer' was. Charlie answered very carefully, "I'm certain that everyone knows that your main objective is the money. After all, I don't believe that the one who took the money is a hardened criminal, but instead, he's probably a person who found himself in a peculiar predicament and reacted—foolishly. But it also seems to me that if I were in the position of the 'old geezer,' I would feel that I couldn't trust the word of any cop or sheriff. I'd want a lot more assurance than someone's word. I'd want something in writing, signed by a judge. Anyway, I don't have to worry about that since I'm not involved." Charlie knew he couldn't tell the sheriff about the treatment that he had received from Bobby Dee and his gang, for then, everything would be exposed and he would go to jail too.

The sheriff continued, "I just wanted to mention that I would appreciate your being willing to spread the word, that I am open to making a deal for any and all pertinent information. Also, I did want to thank you again for all that you did for my daughter, and since you appear to be telling me the truth, I have no more questions at this time. I'll let you go for now, but I might have to call you back later on. Hopefully, you will help me just as I have asked many others, to keep your eyes and ears open as you wander through these mountains."

"Thanks Sheriff—and if you want me, I'll be around for a few more days. I'm staying at Joanne Bott's house for the present and I can run over any time you want me. Please give my regards to your daughter. I'm so happy that everything turned out well for her." With that Charlie arose to leave the police station. As he left the room, he could hear the sheriff announce to his deputies that the whole thing had been a false alarm. "The old boy really didn't know anything. I think maybe he wanted to get a little notoriety, or maybe at his age he felt as if he has been left out of everything that is happening here in Crystal Springs." Charlie mumbled to himself and smiled as he drove toward Joanne's house, "One more hurdle cleared. Now, let's face my next test."

# Eighteen

Early Sunday morning, Charlie and Joanne attempted to put into effect a new plan that he had been piecing together ever since his traumatic meeting with Bobby Dee. Joanne and Charlie acted like teenagers with their new-found love. They talked and discussed all sorts of plans for the whole day. He had even contemplated trading in his old car but decided not to, for that might create more attention and suspicion than he had already generated. But despite the various intricate plans, no final procedure was decided upon.

After Joanne left for work on Monday morning, Charlie quietly sat developing a way to activate his own plan. He took off for Mountain City in order to buy a new disguise. This had to be entirely different from the shaggy old disguise he had used before. This one had to have the appearance of a suave, up-to-date, mature businessman, and yet it must change his look substantially. The first stop he made was to a store that sold wigs and mustaches. The wig he picked was extremely neat and almost looked plastered down, and the mustache was narrow and pointed at the ends. With his teeth in place, his face was no longer hollow looking. No beard was necessary.

The second stop was to a children's store, where he picked up a toy with remote controls. Next, he went to buy a very conservative business suit of good quality. Then on to K-Mart, where he purchased three sheets of poster board and some crayons, and also a flashlight with extra batteries. Before he left for Crystal Springs, he changed into his new business suit, adorned himself with the new wig, and fastened the mustache as well as he could, and at last, he drove to the crossroads where he parked his car.

At this point, he was a little apprehensive that someone might recognize him as he walked past the stores. But his confidence began to soar when he waved to Bobby Dee, with no apparent reaction. He entered Johnny's Restaurant, had pie and coffee and no one paid any attention to him. It was even better than he had hoped.

The only problem he had now was to change back into his every-day clothing and remove the mustache and wig so that even Joanne wouldn't be questioning his actions. Luckily for him, he stopped in the woods and made the change before returning to Joanne's, for she was already home.

Joanne and Charlie then went out for dinner. They picked a restaurant which was quiet and secluded. The conversation revolved mainly about their intimate feelings and also some of their past experiences. At last, Charlie said, "By the way, I called my daughter today and she told me that my brother-in-law who lives near Chattanooga is not doing very well. So she suggested that I run over there to see him tomorrow night. I'll stay for the night, then I'll come back here on Wednesday before I leave on Friday. Is that all right with you? If that's not convenient—"

Joanne never let him finish, "That's fine. Then you won't be here Tuesday night at all?"

"Correct," answered Charlie, as they made their way through the back roads to home.

Early Tuesday morning, Joanne and Charlie said goodbye as Joanne went off to work. "I won't see you until sometime Wednesday afternoon, right?" asked Joanne.

"Yes, I'll be here about an hour or so today before I leave 'cause I have to make a few local phone calls. So I'll see you Wednesday afternoon."

After careful thought, Charlie picked up the phone and called the *Crystal Springs Chronicle,* the local weekly newspaper. He asked to speak to the production manager and was quickly connected to Mr. Belcher. "Sir, I'm interested in running a large ad in your paper. It would be a one-page insert but it would have to be delivered tomorrow with your regular issue."

"Sir," said the production manager, "it's getting late for this issue. Perhaps we could run it for you next week."

"Now, Mr. Belcher, I'm willing to pay double your normal price if you will put it in this week."

"Well, that makes it more possible, doesn't it? When could I expect to get the copy? Mister—I didn't get your name."

"My name is Chet Crawley, and the earliest that I can give you the copy would be by 6 A.M. Wednesday."

"If I know the amount of space that you'll need that would be alright. As you probably know, we print the inserts and then, we need a little time to collate them with the regular issue. We put the papers in the news rack around twelve noon. Now, as for payment, I'd have to require the money in advance."

"Certainly, I shall bring the money to your office before 5:30 P.M. tonight. Is that satisfactory?"

"That's fine, Mr. Crawley, Miss Woods will have the bill and you can pay her. However, let me caution you, Mr. Crawley, if we do not receive the copy by six in the morning, the insert will not be printed."

"Thank you, Mr. Belcher. I appreciate your help."

After the arrangements were set, Charlie sat at the dining room table gluing a message on the poster board that he had bought at K-Mart. His first message was called, "Instructions No. 1." Then with the next poster board, a new message was called "Instructions No. 2." The first poster board was folded and securely attached to the remote control toy that he had purchased in Mountain City. The second, Charlie folded and inserted into a bag and tied it with a long cord that could be used to hang the bag in a tree. With the completion of the instructions, Charlie wrote a long note to Joanne which he left open, for he wanted to put something in it at the last moment. By the time he had accomplished all of his preliminary tasks, the time was approaching the 5:30 P.M. deadline of his appointment. So Charlie made a quick trip to the waterfalls to get some cash for payment to the newspaper, and then dressed himself in his new businessman's disguise with the smooth hair and the neat mustache and his new suit.

He arrived at the *Crystal Springs Chronicle's* office at exactly 5:20 P.M. as Miss Woods was preparing to close up.

"Miss Woods, I'm Mr. Crawley. I spoke with your Mr. Belcher this morning about running an insert in your paper tomorrow."

"Yes, Mr. Crawley. He told me all about it. Here is your invoice."

Charlie looked at the bill and then handed Miss Woods an envelope. "I think you'll find the amount in this envelope will more than cover your invoice."

"Mr. Crawley, this is more than double the amount of Mr. Belcher's invoice. This is much too much."

"No, that's alright. That's what we agreed, so that I'd be certain that your company won't fail me tomorrow. I promised to deliver the copy at exactly 6 A.M. tomorrow. Do you know who will be here to take my call?"

"Mr. Belcher will take your call personally."

"And you're sure your company won't let me down?"

"I'm sure, sir. Mr. Belcher was very definite in his instructions."

Charlie thanked her and returned to his car. He drove to a small restaurant where he enjoyed supper by himself and mentally prepared himself for a long night of hard work.

As dusk fell, Charlie drove to the woods near the waterfall, where he had hidden the ice chests. With his flashlight and his shovel he made his way though the woods, across the log over the small stream, up the hill to his hiding spot near the waterfall. He spent several minutes removing the branches and brush that hid the ice chests. He then dug up the ice chests and checked them one by one. Everything was in perfect order, except some of the money that he had taken for the newspaper for his expenses, and some money that he put in his letter to Joanne.

For the next couple of hours, Charlie worked furiously, carrying each ice chest out of the woods one by one to the car. The chests seem to get heavier as the hours went by, especially for a man of eighty. When all the chests were jammed in the car, Charlie drove to the new place that he had selected to hide the money. He parked the car near the dam at the north end of Lake Arrowhead.

The overflow area was dry at this time of year, so Charlie carried all of the chests down the hill and stashed the ice chests on top of each other. They couldn't be seen from the dam or the approaching road. Charlie took a lot of time and a lot of care stacking the ice chests under the old bridge against the dam. When Charlie saw the headlights of a car coming around the bend, he stopped and turned off his flashlight until the car passed. By the time everything was in its place, Charlie had worked almost all night. His back ached and he was exhausted. There were only a few things left to do. He hung the second poster board with the cord in a tree a short distance from the dam and in an odd position overhanging a small cliff. It was not easy to get to, but one could reach it. Next, he took the clothes and all the disguises that he had used during the robbery and stuffed them until the shape resembled the 'old geezer.' Then he placed the dummy on the ice chests as if he were guarding the money.

At last, Charlie had almost everything in place, and all he had to do now was to call the newspaper at precisely 6 A.M. and then take his position. At this point he only had a couple of hours to sleep, and the only place he could sleep was in the back seat of his car. He was tired and very restless and he laughed to himself because it had been many, many years since he had been in a back seat—and never alone!

As he shut his eyes in hopes of sleeping a little, he thought how fortunate it was that he hadn't moved the money from the hiding place near the waterfall to his new choice, the storage cellar at the burned-out Owens' barn. It would have taken a lot longer to move all the money and the ice chests and in addition, Charlie knew that he was more exposed in that valley. The possibility of being seen by someone like Franklin Delano Roose was very great and that would ruin his whole plan. At least, he had saved himself a lot of extra work and luckily, the children who played near the waterfalls never discovered the money anyway. To transfer all his hidden treasures from the waterfalls to the dam expended all the energy that his eighty years of age would allow. He fell asleep immediately.

# Nineteen

Charlie woke at the first sign of light. He was still tired but at least he felt confident that he could make his plan work. Today was going to be a busy day. He drove to the shopping mart and used the outside pay phone to make his call to the *Crystal Springs Chronicle*. It was exactly 6 A.M. when he made his call. "Mr. Belcher? This is Chet Crawley."

"Good morning, sir, how are you today? I've been awaiting your call. But before you give me the copy, I would like you to know that you paid more than I expected for your insert."

"Yes, I realize that, but I wanted to be positive that your company would do exactly as I ask," Charlie answered.

"We will honor our word, so now please give me the copy."

"Okay. Here it is. I would like the following in headlines, Mr. Belcher.

*COME ONE, COME ALL*
*TREASURE HUNT*
*MILLIONS AT STAKE.*

*Your first set of instructions will be delivered to you at precisely 1:00 P.M. at Dick's Landing on Route 17 in Lake Shores on Lake Arrowhead.*
*Come One, Come All.*
*Do not attempt to arrive earlier as the instructions will not be given until 1:00 P.M. This is a treasure hunt for the benefit of you and everyone in your town. There are millions of dollars at stake."*

"That's it, Mr. Belcher, That's all I want." Mr. Belcher repeated the entire message, and then said suspiciously, "Supposing I don't put this in the paper? I didn't think this had anything to do with the stolen money, 'til you gave me this copy."

"Sir, if you don't do as you promised, you will not get the set of instructions at Dick's Landing or any other instructions that you might need in order to locate the treasure. The result should be obvious. Another thing, Mr. Belcher, I don't want to see anyone taking advantage of getting the information early and arriving at Dick's Landing ahead of anyone else. It's necessary to have many people find the treasure at the same time. The more people we have, the safer it'll be. And as you can easily see, the entire town will benefit when it is returned, not just a few. I promise you, Mr. Belcher, if you do not do as I have asked, no one will ever see the money again. Goodbye, sir."

Charlie, immediately, hung up the phone and drove to the time share to have breakfast with his fishing friend, Jeff. Both men reminisced about their fishing and made plans to do more fishing together, next year. The conversation naturally turned to the robbery but neither had any new news or anything definitive to say. Finally, Charlie verified the fact that he was leaving immediately for home. He was all packed and wouldn't be here in town more than 10 minutes more. "I'll be back next year, then maybe we can get in plenty of good fishing. And maybe by then, the town won't be so overcrowded, because the robbery will have been solved by then."

The two men shook hands and bade each other goodbye, and Charlie drove toward Lake Arrowhead. He wanted to position himself on the peninsula long before any traffic would arrive at Dick's Landing. From the place he picked on the peninsula, he could easily see Dick's Landing, and with a little care he could hide himself so that no one could possibly see him. It was a perfect place. Charlie lay down under two large pine trees where he could operate a remote control unit. The site was very close to a short path that would lead him back to his car which was hidden behind some bushes. This position would afford him an easy exit to the south lane of Route 17, which was his planned escape route in the opposite direction of the heavy traffic.

At a quarter to one, the newspaper trucks were on their appointed rounds to put the newspapers in the racks and to deliver some of them to stores and restaurants. One of the drivers was tipping off everyone by saying, "Hey man, you better check out this paper; there's something special in it today!" Some of the locals who were eating lunch grabbed a copy of the weekly newspaper and screamed as they saw the insert. Their voices rose in a matter of moments and the word spread like wind-blown fire.

It only took a few minutes for the cars, trucks, and every variety of transportation to head towards Lake Arrowhead. Even the police were headed north. It became necessary for the police to direct traffic through the crossroads going north.

Almost at once, there was a traffic jam in the parking lot near Dick's Landing. Hundreds of people were gathering at the docks. Even the shoreline was packed with people. The talking grew louder and louder. The crowd was becoming unruly, until at last, the cops began to demand some order. Speculation was on everyone's lips. "Treasure Hunt? Millions? What the hell were they talking about? What money? Could it really be millions of dollars?"

The sheriff arrived to work his way through the crowd to the main dock, and with a foghorn in hand he attempted to quiet the crowd. But at exactly one o'clock the entire crowd, numbering in the hundreds, became quiet of their own accord. Everyone scoured the horizon, but nothing was in view.

It didn't take long for the crowd to become restless, when suddenly someone screamed, "Look over there! What's that coming around the bend of the lake? It's a toy boat and it's coming straight for the dock."

A toy boat was heading directly toward the dock and was moving rapidly. Charlie with his remote control maneuvered the little speed- boat around the point of land and it headed directly toward the dock.

The sheriff asked, "Who's controlling it? Someone's running it by remote control, but where are they? Can anyone see who's operating that boat?"

The shouting was unbelievable, until the sheriff blew his whistle to gain some order. He announced over his foghorn that the crowd must calm down until the boat reached the dock. As the boat continued toward the dock, correcting its path from time to time, one could see a roll of poster board sticking out of the back of the toy boat.

As the boat reached the dock, a deputy leaned out to retrieve the poster board. "Quiet! Quiet, please!" the sheriff blasted over the foghorn. "I'll read it out loud to all of you at the same time."

The sheriff opened the poster board and began to read over the foghorn. "Instruction number one: Go to the end of Dam Lake."

Someone yelled, "To the end of the dam lake? What the hell does that mean? Which end?"

Quickly, it dawned on many minds at the same time. "The dam end!" The end that has a dam. And then, almost in unison, as if it had been choreographed, the people bolted to their vehicles to drive north to the dam.

A massive traffic jam ensued, not only on the road going north, but in the wooded area around the dam where everyone wanted to park. They pulled their cars over the bridge near the spillway to park in every available spot near the dumpster. The people were assembling near the dam with a fervor that was hard to control. Again, the sheriff had to push his way through the crowd until he saw a large arrow painted on the tree pointing toward the edge of the Cliffs.

Meanwhile, Charlie, who had stationed himself on the peninsula in order to control his toy boat, left his hide-out and calmly walked to his car. For a moment or two, he watched the heavy traffic moving along the road north, then he drove south toward Crystal Springs and its Crossroads and turned off the main road toward Joanne's home. He wanted to pickup some clothing and leave a letter for Joanne.

At the same time, a long way away from Charlie, through the mountains and across the lake, the people were scrambling to find the final instructions to the location of the fortune. Never, in the history of North Carolina, had there been a traffic jam that could compare to this. The treasure hunters searched the parking area and the woods, and at last, they followed the sheriff to the cliff.

"There it is hanging in the tree. Can we reach it?" the sheriff said.

One of the bigger deputies stretched out and finally gathered in the bag which contained the poster board. He questioned,

"Why do you suppose they put this in such a difficult place to reach?"

"Oh, I think it's obvious that they wanted some extra time. But we don't know what they needed it for as yet," Sheriff Macklin said.

At last, the bag was opened and instruction number two was read to the crowd.

"Quiet please," the sheriff called over the foghorn. "Look under the bridge where the dry spillway begins. You will behold more treasure than you have ever seen in your life. It is being guarded by an 'old Geezer.' Be careful, walk up to him quietly and with caution, as he is a fragile old man. Please take your time for this is Crystals Springs' legacy. You must return this fortune to its rightful owners, then your town will be blessed forever."

Almost at once, everyone ran for the dry spillway. The people who were leading the way slowed down when they saw the old man sitting on one of the ice chests. He was sitting there with his head slightly bent and he looked weird in his wig and beard, and he was dressed in his dirty old mountain clothes.

But the closer the people got, the more they realized it was just a bunch of old clothes stuffed to look like a person. Next to the 'old geezer' was another poster board that read as follows: "Here is your money, or at least most of it. Please return it to its rightful owners. Do not make the mistake of keeping it for yourselves. Your town now has a history that will draw visitors and sightseers for a century. Enjoy your legacy."

The sheriff posted his deputies around the ice chests, while he and couple of assistants inspected each and every one of them. The money was there. It looked like there was millions of dollars, all neatly stacked in the chests.

The crowd had quieted down. It was mumbling rather than yelling. Some of the people walked close to the 'old geezer' as if to be certain that he wasn't a human. By this time, the FBI had arrived, and of course they wanted to take control of the situation. Sheriff Macklin suddenly declared that no one, including the FBI, had any jurisdiction in this circumstance other than the sheriff himself. "So back off," he demanded. "You will all be a witness to this event. And I shall follow the instructions to the letter. Everything will be done in accordance with the law." The crowd showed their respect by obeying his every command.

When the sheriff had finished reading the instructions to the treasure hunters, he became aware of a small note that was slipped between the folds. It was addressed to him personally. He quickly turned his back to the crowd so that he could read it without being noticed.

The note read: *"Congratulations on the recovery of the money and the capture of the bank robbers but if you — STILL — wish final closure to the case, search the mountains above the waterfalls and have a long 'fireside chat' with FDR!"* Sheriff Macklin stood for a moment, questioning two things, "Why was 'still' separated, and who was FDR?" It took but a split second for him to realize that the writer meant a moonshiner's STILL and that FDR referred to Franklin Delano Roose.

While this was happening, Charlie had arrived at Joanne's house. He still had a key so he had easy access. He gathered his remaining clothes, then placed the key on top of the letter that he had left for Joanne. Attached to the letter was a small piece of a fake mustache, and in the envelope he placed twenty-five thousand dollars. The note that he left read as follows:

*Darling,*

> *First, I want to tell you that I love you very much. I have changed our plans once again, but this time I'm sure that you will be well satisfied. I'm following your philosophy: If they come in the front door, we'll walk out the back. The sheriff, Bobby Dee, and the FBI were all coming in the front — since our discussion, I have gone through a metamorphosis. I started off thinking that my most important concern was to leave a big legacy to my children. Next, I felt that love could conquer all problems. Now, I realize that both of these can only be enjoyed when everything else fits into the straight and narrow path of an honest conscience. You were right when you said "No." Now at last, I have come to my senses. I can't run away either, and I realize that I must be honest and truthful. So here is my new scheme. Today, I returned the money, all but a small amount. I hope you can use this token to help your daughter. I'm glad we both agree that there are times in life when some*

*things are better untold and this seems to be one of them.*
*Joanne, I am now leaving for home to put my life in order so*
*that when I return I can ask you to marry me under normal,*
*ordinary, and sane circumstances. I love you very much, and I*
*will be back very soon. I Promise.*

*Charlie*

Charlie had planned it well. By the time Joanne had arrived
home and opened the envelope, she would realize that Charlie,
the 'old geezer,' had followed his conscience to return the money.
And perhaps, by that time, the TV would be reporting that the
money had been recovered. No one would be arrested and most
of the residents would be happy.

Charlie knew that his secret was secure. Joanne wouldn't be
able to return the money he'd left for her, because then she'd be
involved in the whole affair. It could end exactly as Charlie had
hoped.

Next, Charlie headed down the road where he had met
Franklin Delano Roose, near Owens' burned-out barn. He
stopped near the tree with a huge hole in the trunk. He
remembered that Franklin was using this tree as his private mail
box. Charlie took out a piece of paper and wrote a note.

"Franklin, don't drink it, use it for food. Your old friend."
Then he put a thousand dollars with his note in an envelope. He
put Franklin's name on it and dropped it into the hollow tree.
Charlie realized that his note was not enough, so he added a
short letter.

*Dear Franklin,*

*Your instincts were right but don't judge me too harshly. I*
*set out on the tortuous path up the dark side of the mountain*
*though a maze of turns and dead ends which were blackened by*
*the shadows of doubt and indecision. But when I arrived at the*
*summit to look down the glistening side, this path was*
*brightened by the sunlight of honesty and dignity, I knew that*
*I must descend step by step to the shining green valley below.*
*The valley was crystal-like from the glow of decency and*
*truthfulness. It was my true destination. It was the only path*

*available to me. I feel better for having returned all the recently discovered fortune.*

*Keep up your quotations and maintain your independence.*

*Your look-a-like and moonshine-sipping friend*

As soon as Charlie had accomplished these two errands, he headed toward High Prairie. He congratulated himself on how well everything was working out—the sheriff was left with a feeling that he had accomplished a tremendously successful job. He had captured the crooks and he had gotten the money back with no one being hurt. The crowds, the townsfolk, and all the local residents had experienced a real treasure hunt which turned into the largest block party in the mountains. The town had a wonderful legacy. The insurance companies would have little to complain about for they had gotten back the overwhelming majority of the money. The merchants never had any greater sales and the town would undoubtedly prosper for years. The tourists would come to see the actual bank and area of one of the biggest robberies in history. Lastly, Joanne could help her daughter and grandchildren and still have Charlie propose marriage. Even old Franklin could enjoy a bottle of gin with his meal.

Charlie felt especially good, for his name and reputation was still untarnished. His kids still respected him and he felt that finally he had done the right thing. It certainly was better to give than to receive, especially since he was giving something that wasn't even his. He was certain that Ethel would be proud of him after all, or if not proud, at least, if she asked, "Can you live with this?" He could answer "Yes."

As he drove toward High Prairie, Charlie admitted to himself that this had been one hell of a busy day. It was almost three o'clock and he was hungry. He decided to stop at the drug store for a sandwich. How nice it would be to sit with no cares and read the newspaper. He took a sip of coffee and turned to the second page of the paper, because the first page was nothing but stories about the robbery. The first glance at the headlines was "Unclaimed Lottery Tickets." As he casually read the article, he understood that the winners were located in this section of the mountains but they had not come forth to claim their prize. After finishing his sandwich and coffee, Charlie paid his bill, then climbed into his car to start his long trip home. He tried to remember where he'd put the lottery tickets that he had bought. At last, it dawned on him, he had put them in the dash box of his car. He reached the dash box and pulled out the tickets. Charlie looked at them once, then looked away. He looked again and then a third time. Finally, he grabbed the newspaper and compared the numbers again.

At last he said, "My God, I've won the lottery!"